DOT-TO-DOODLE™
MANDALAS
TO DRAW AND COLOUR

First published in the United Kingdom in 2016 by

Portico

1 Gower Street

London

WC1E 6HD

An imprint of Pavilion Books Company Ltd

ISBN 978-1-911042-49-5

A CIP catalogue record for this book is available from the British Library.

10 9 8 7 6 5 4 3 2 1

Reproduction by Mission Productions Ltd, Hong Kong

Printed and bound by C.O.S. Printers Pte Ltd, Singapore

This book can be ordered direct from the publisher at www.pavilionbooks.com

DOT-TO-DOODLE™
MANDALAS
TO DRAW AND COLOUR

PORTICO

How to create

You can copy the beautiful mandalas in this book using this dot-to-doodle method.
It's easy, fun and challenging – the designs get more complex as you work your way through the book!
At the back of this book there are some extra templates so that you can design and doodle mandalas of
your own. You can colour or stipple your designs when they are complete.

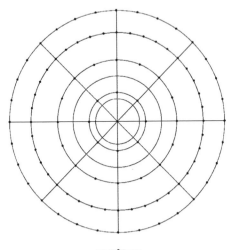

step one

Carefully study the mandala design on the left hand side of the
book to see how the pattern connects using the dots and circular
template as guides.

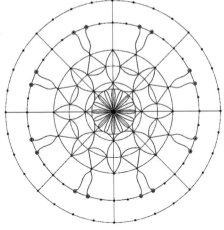

step two

Starting with a pencil and at the centre of the template, begin to
copy out the design using the dots and circles to gauge the shapes
and their dimensions within the design. Look out for the intersecting
lines in the mandala as they are also useful guides. Begin with the
main shapes, leaving the detail for later.

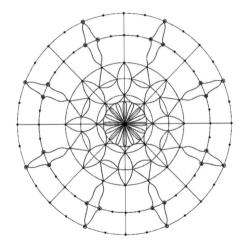

step three

Working from the centre outwards, complete the main outlines of
the design. Once the basic pattern is in place, start adding the detail
within – you can keep copying the finished mandala or add patterns
of your own.

step four

When you are happy with your design, go over it with ink and rub out any pencil marks for a cleaner look.

step five

Now your mandala is ready to colour – or try stippling instead by creating a pattern using varying degrees of shading using small dots.

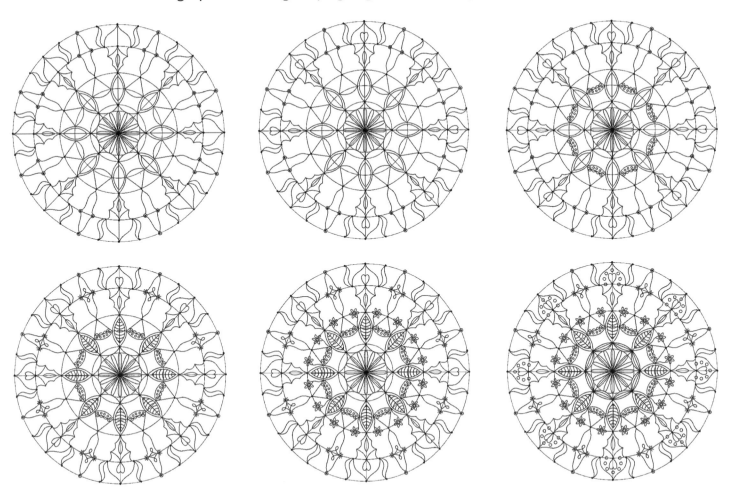

Tip: A ruler and compass might come in handy for those that like a very precise look.

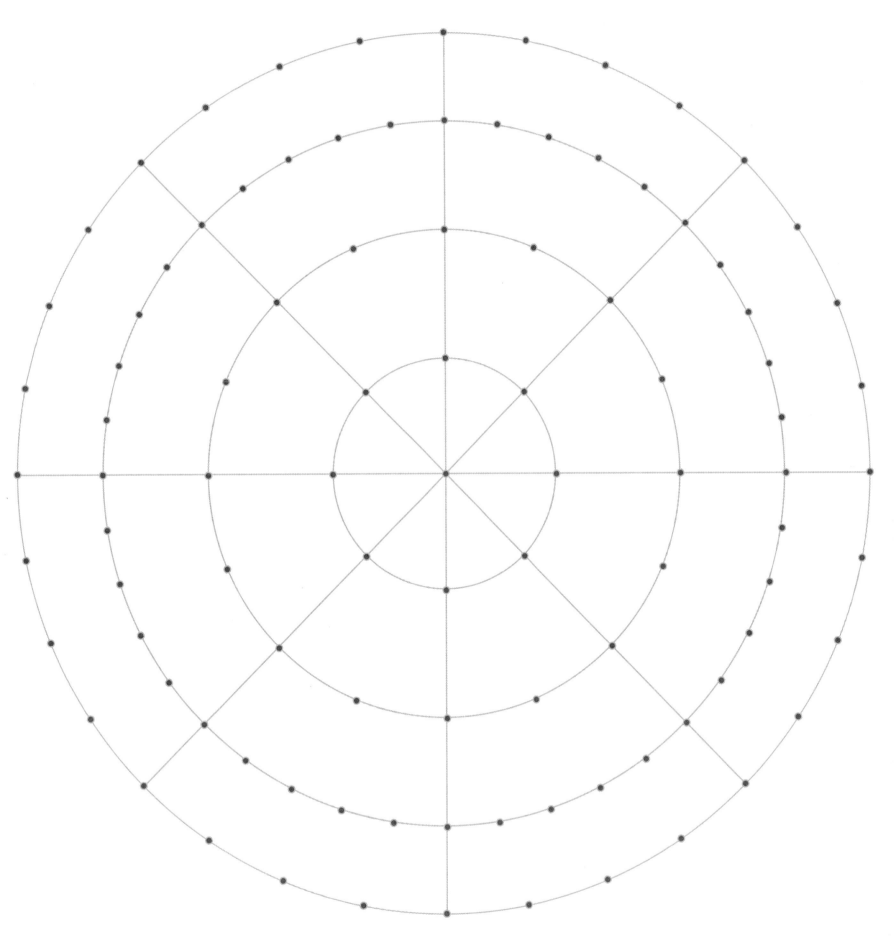

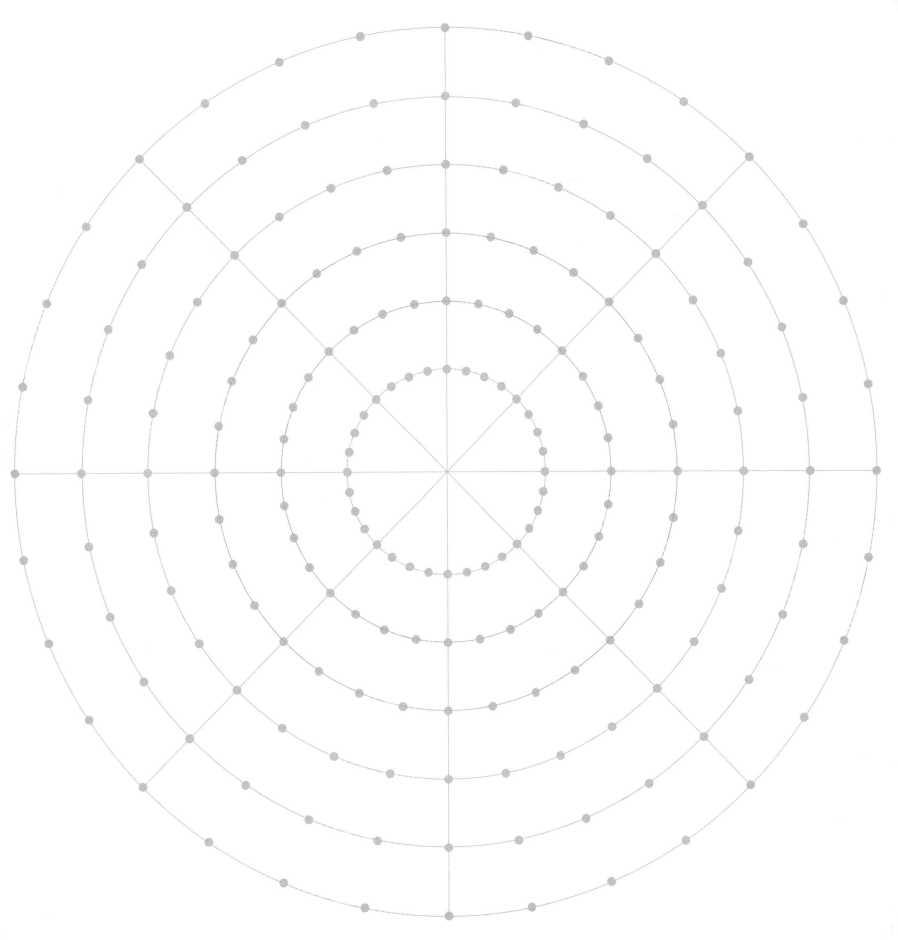

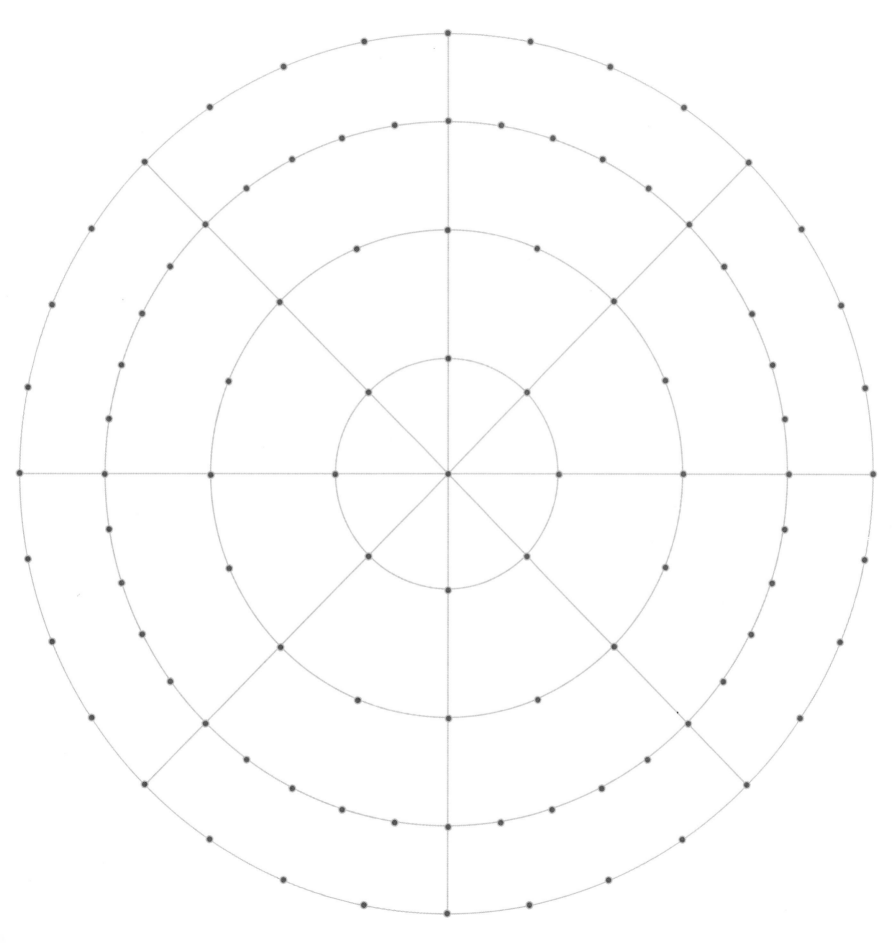

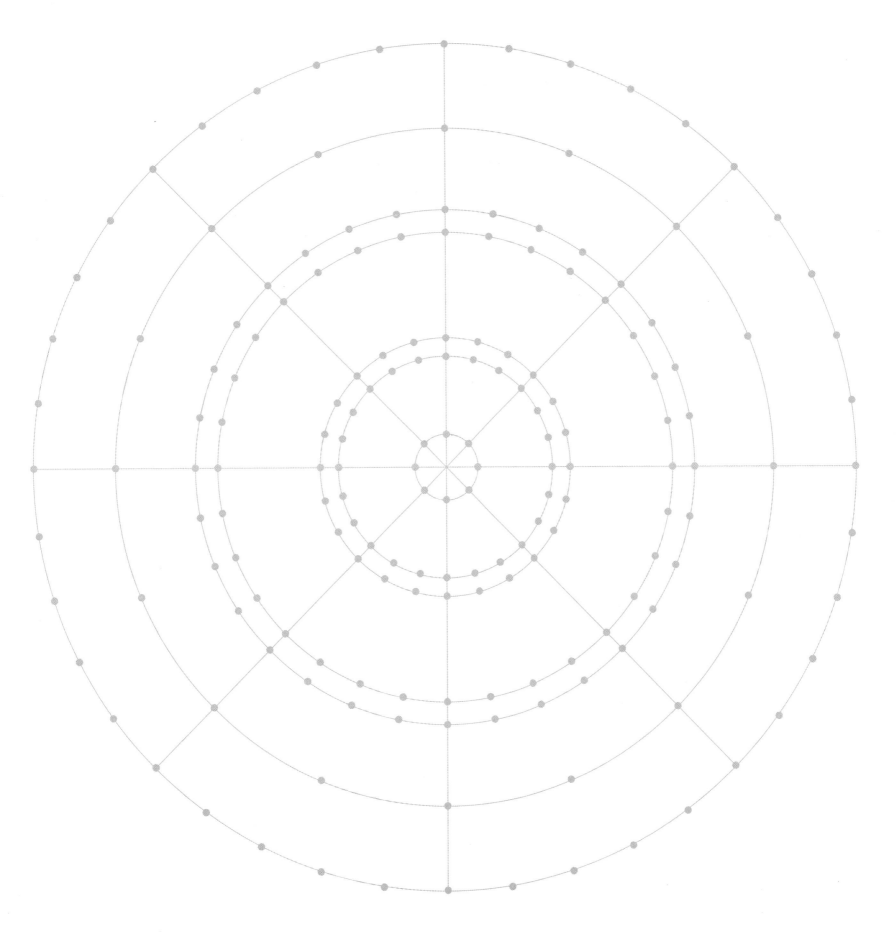

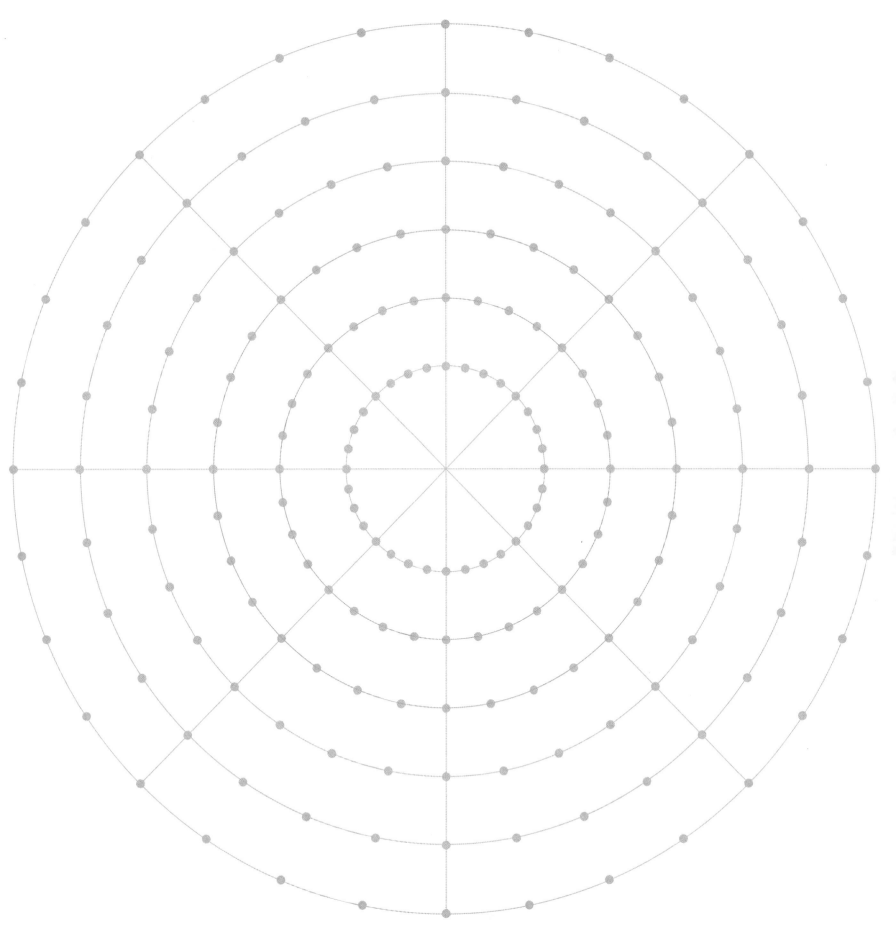

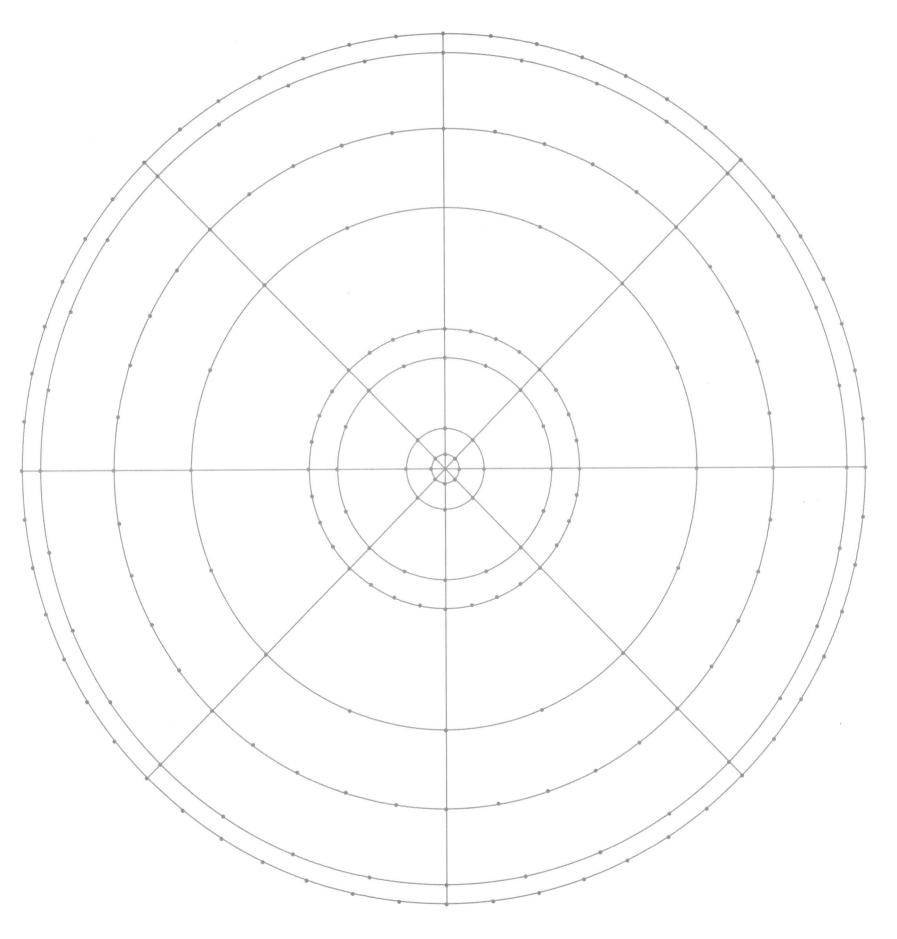

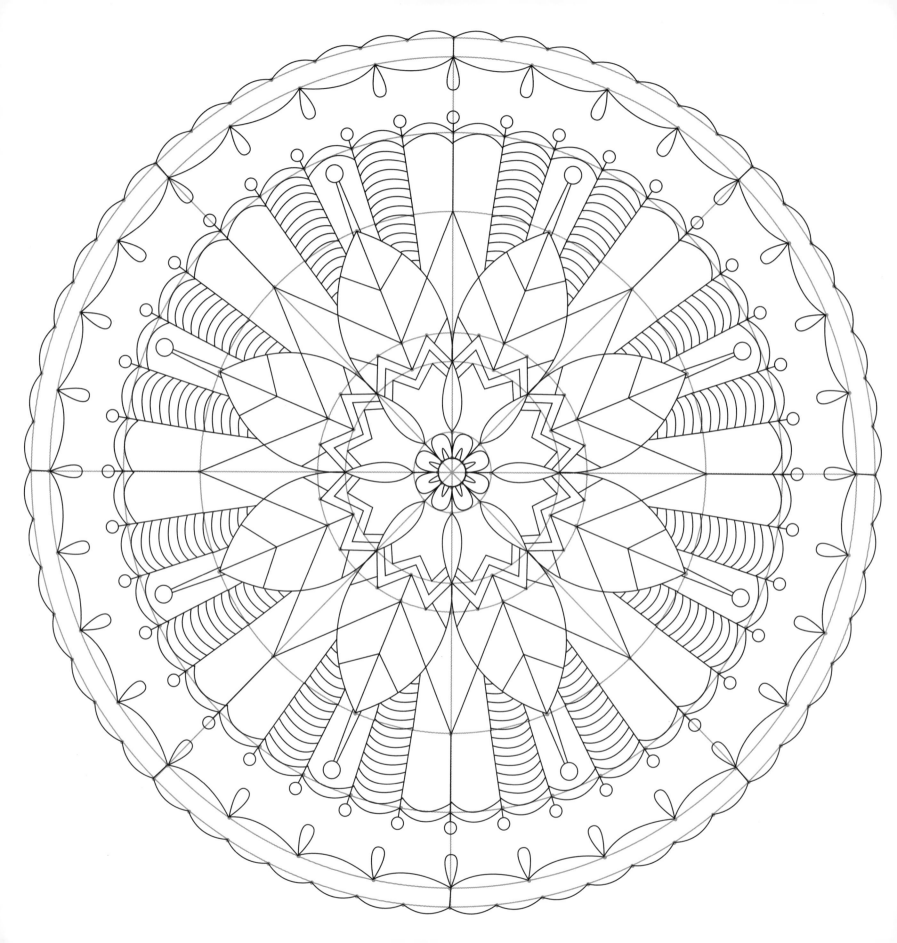

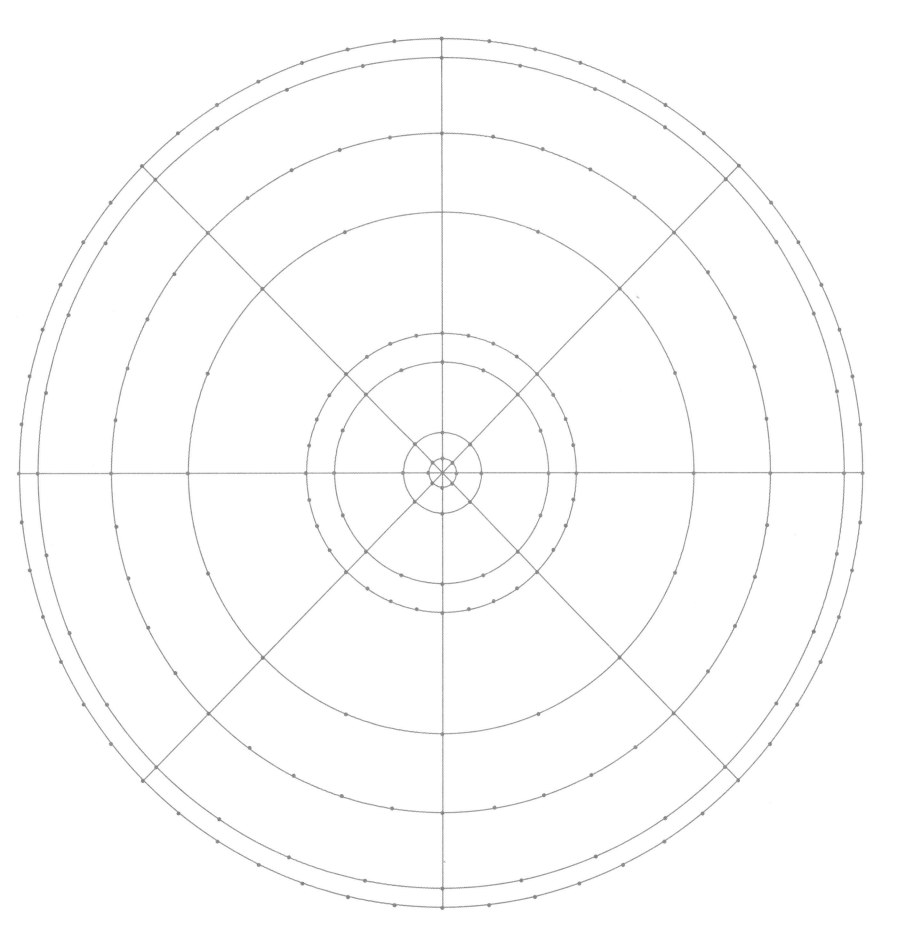

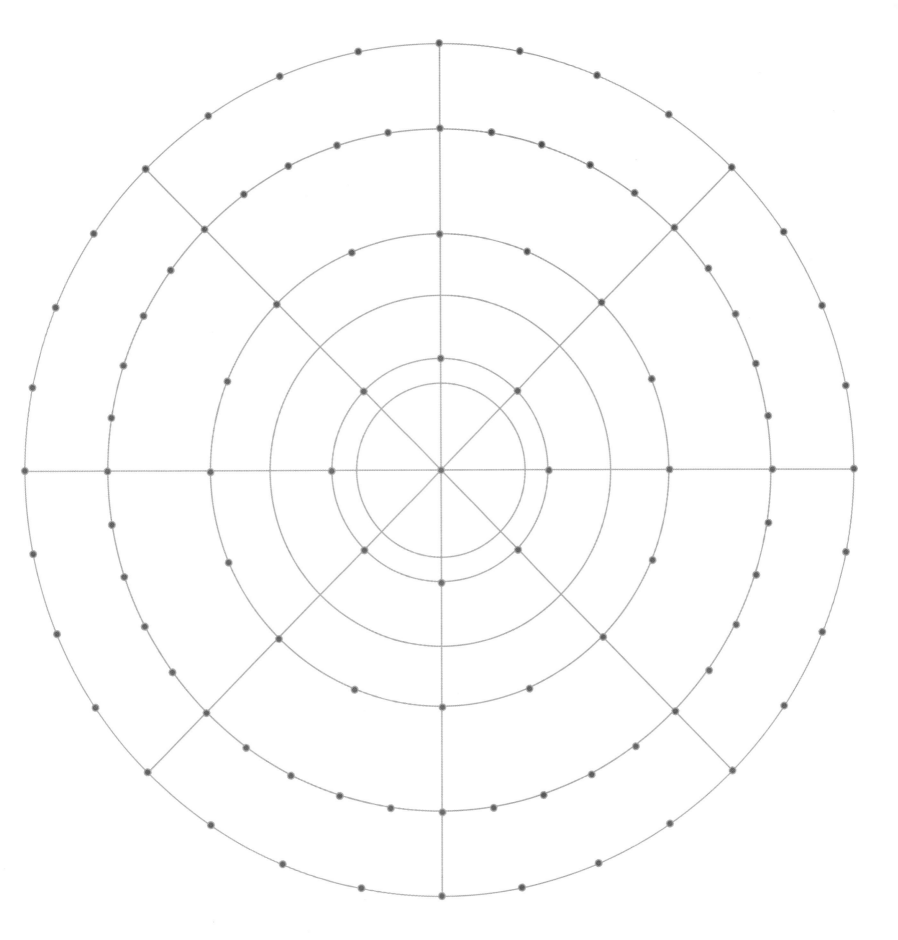

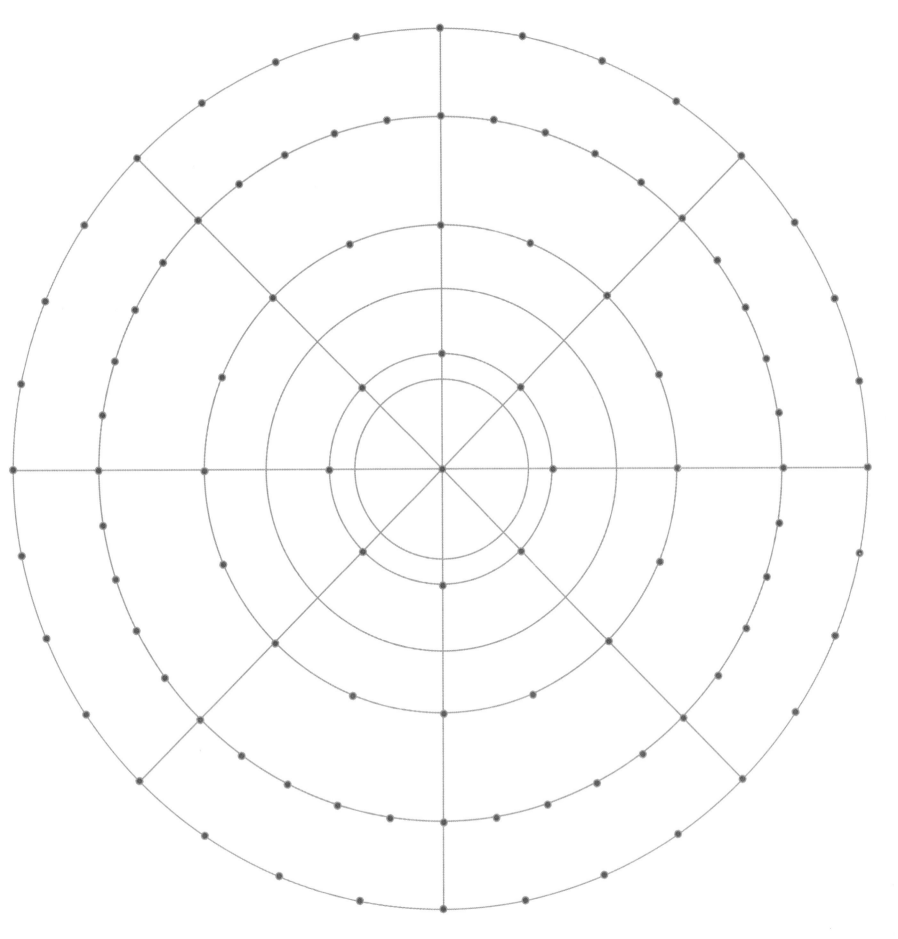

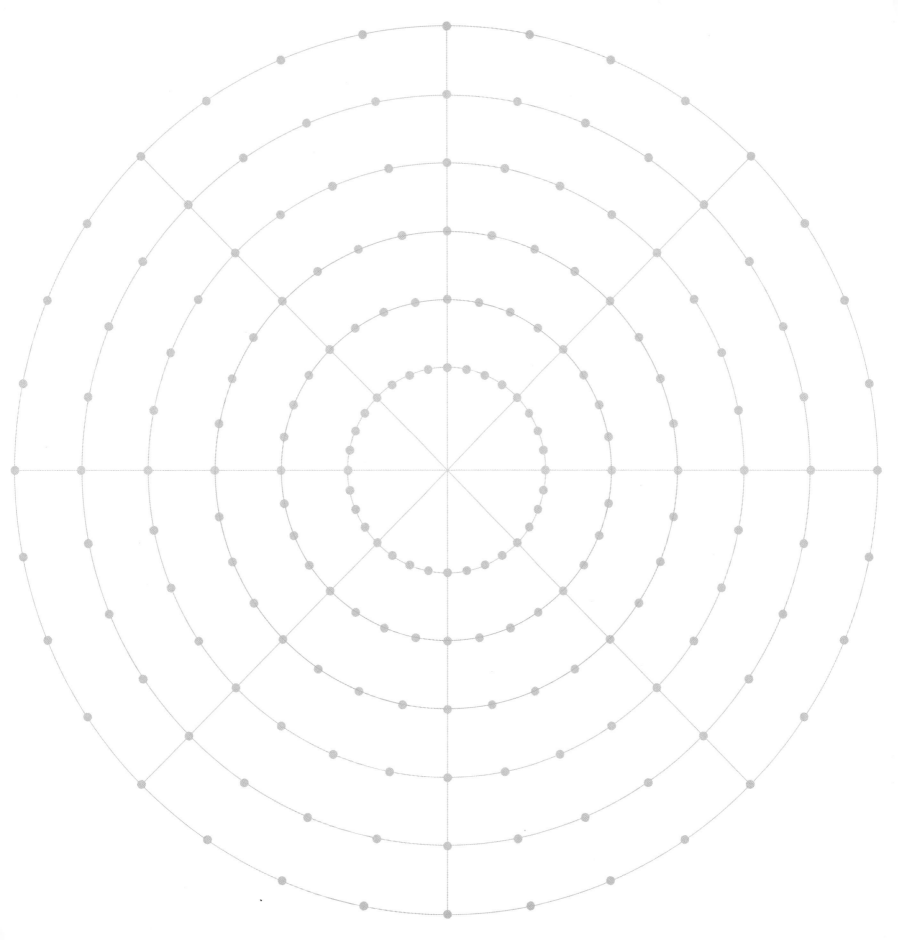

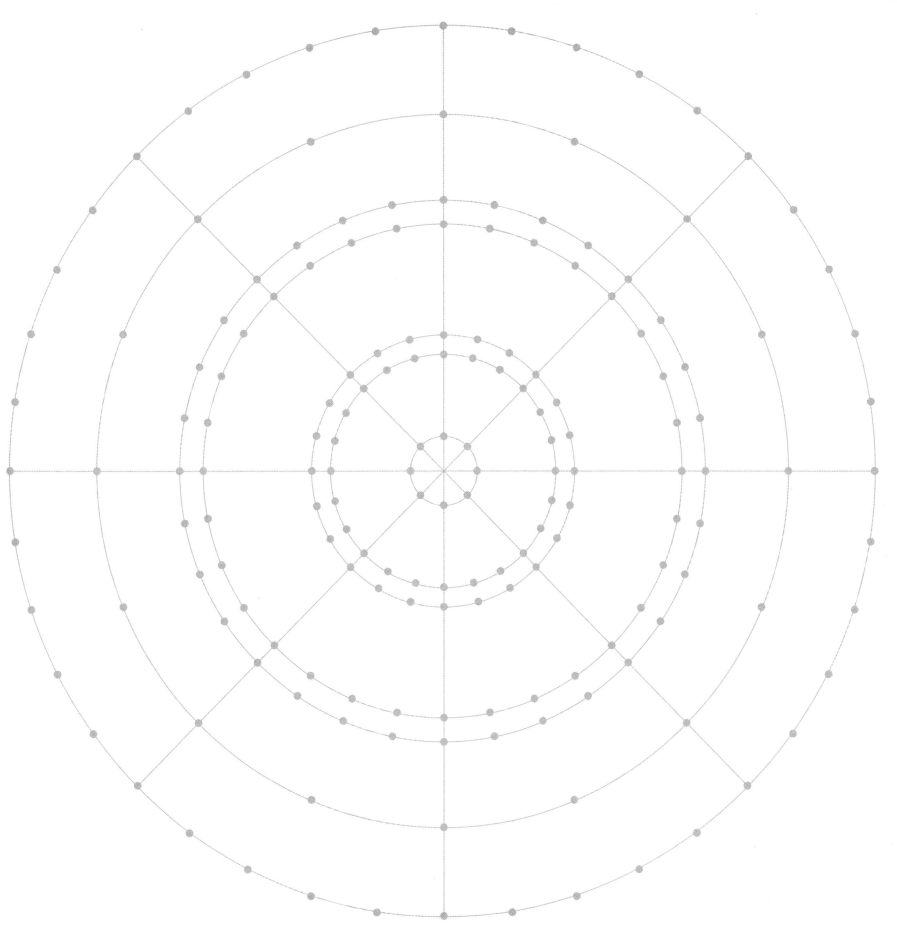

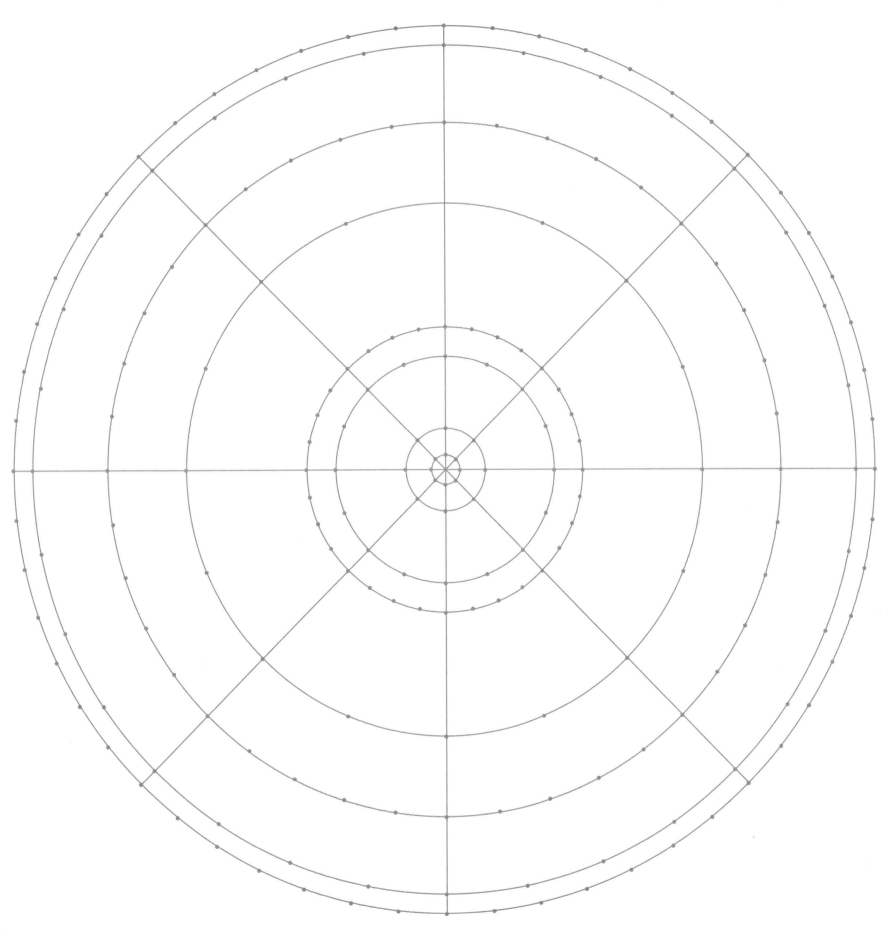

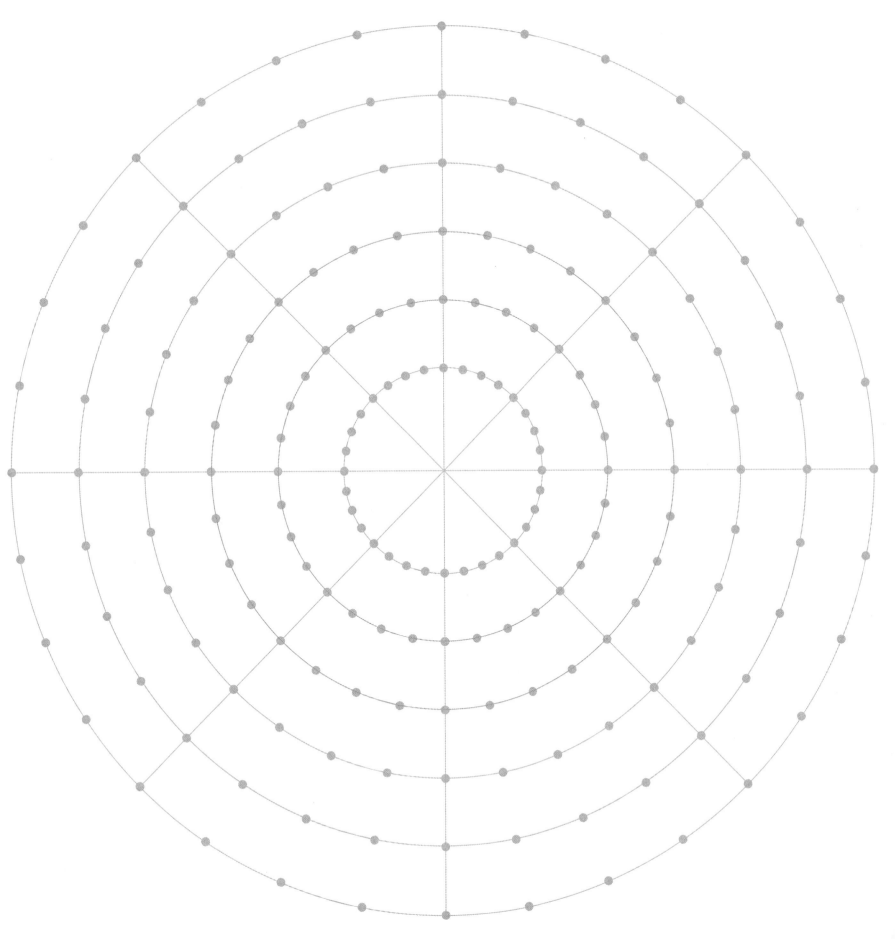

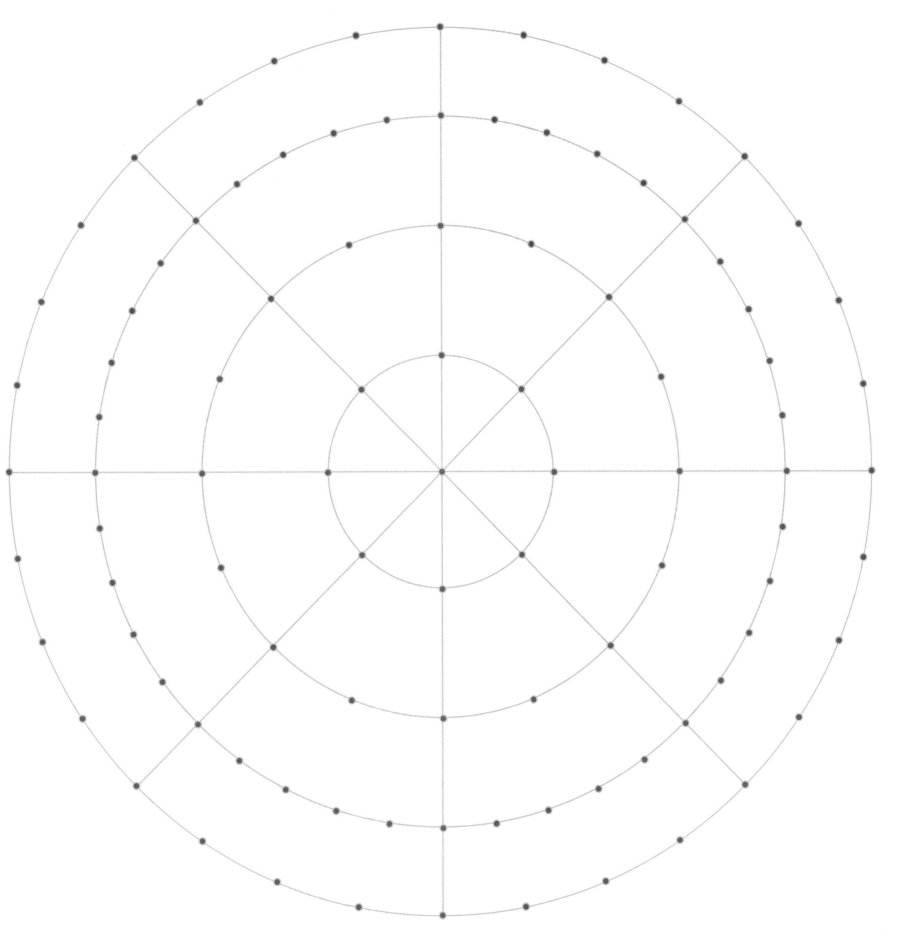

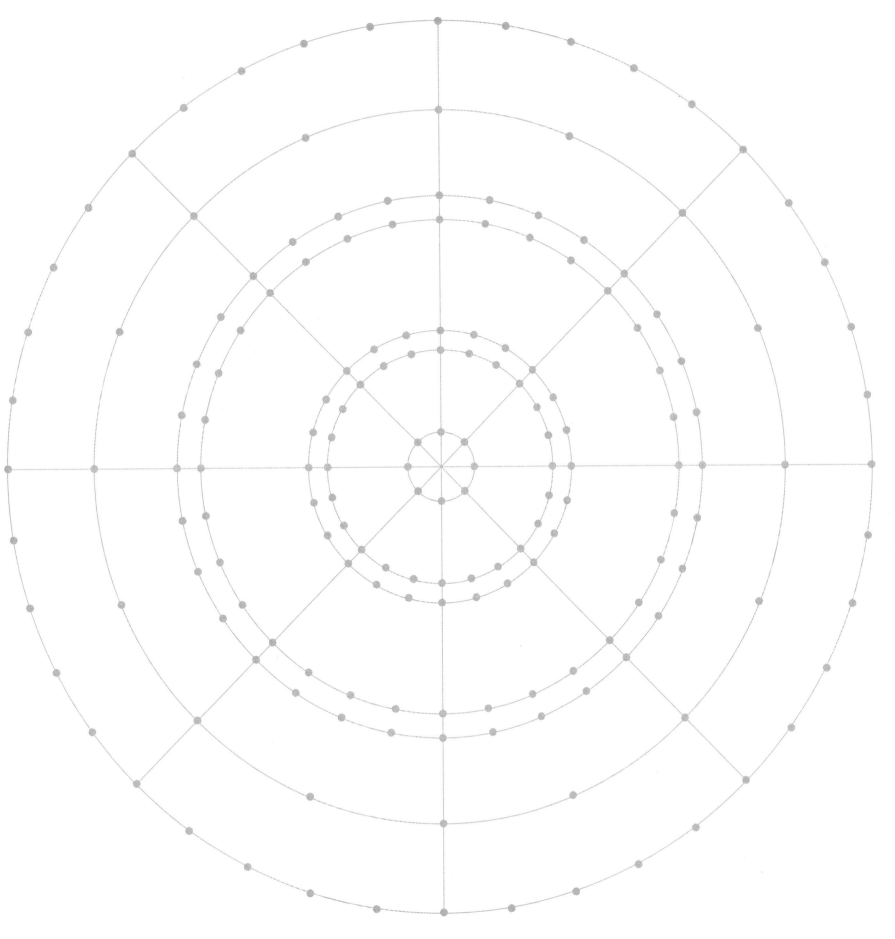

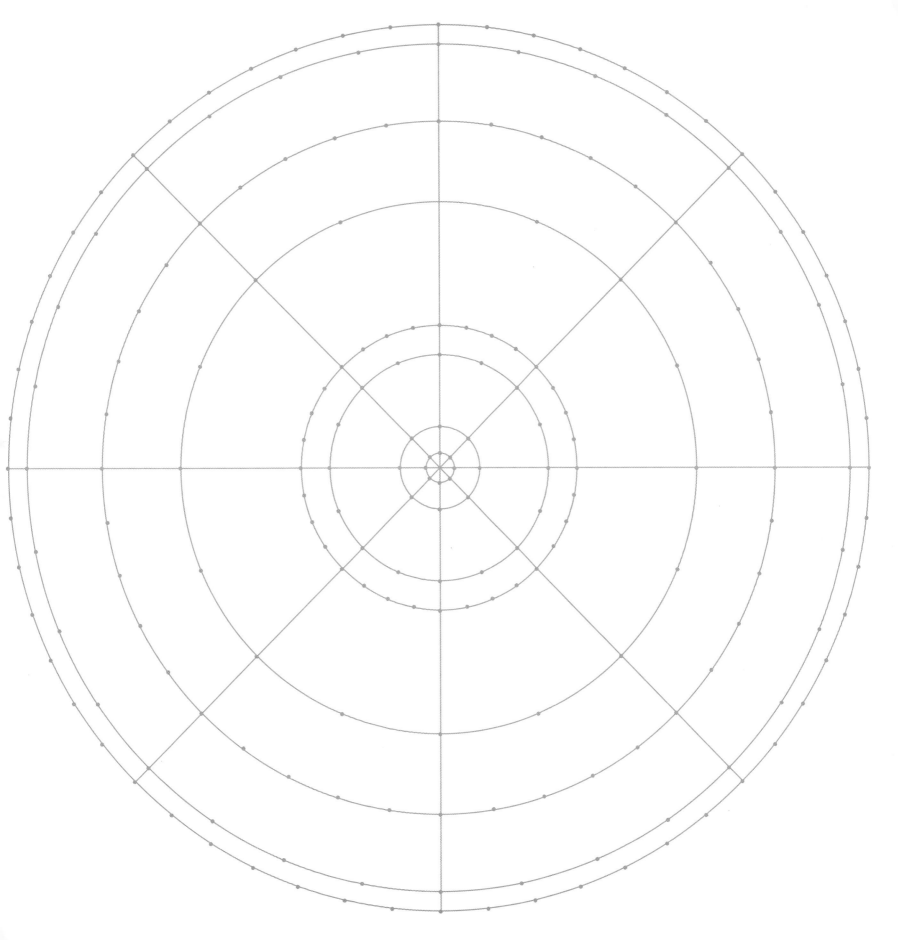

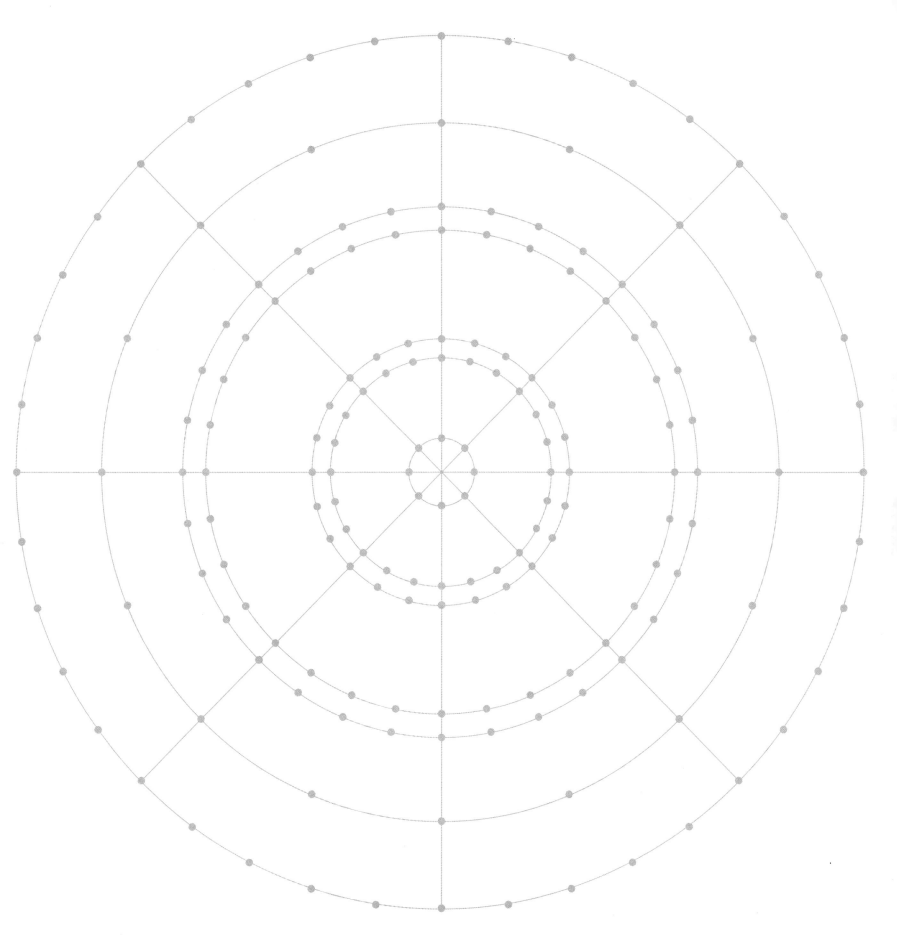

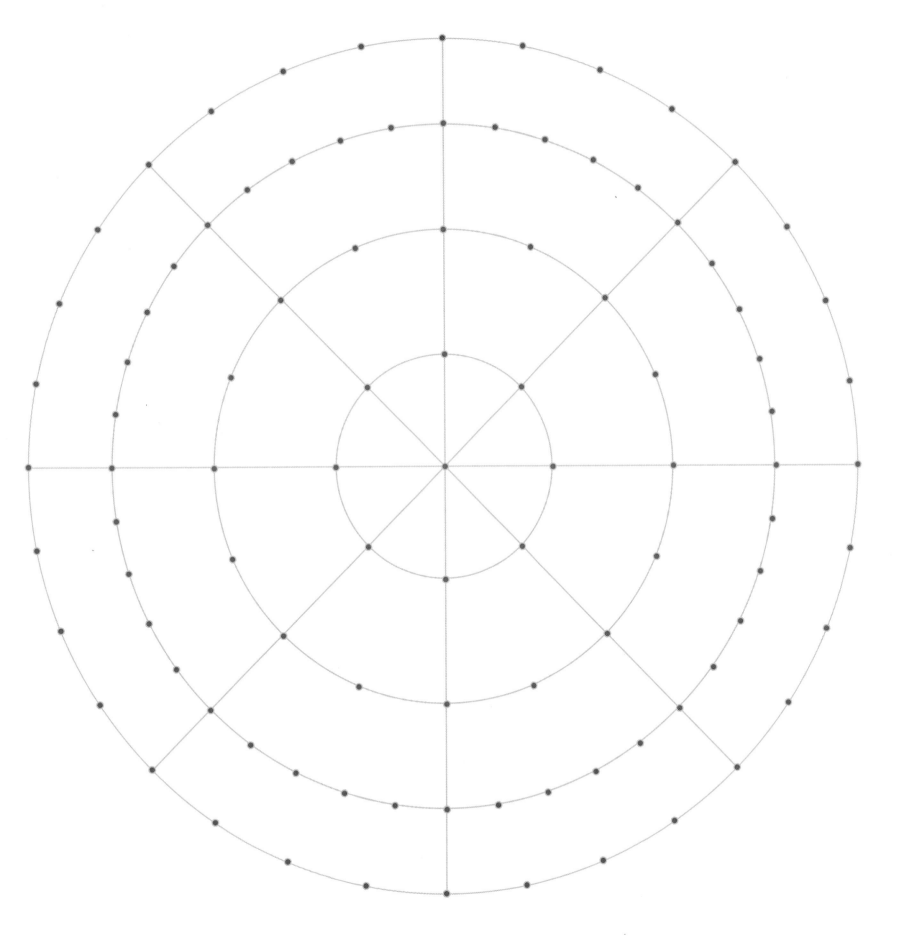

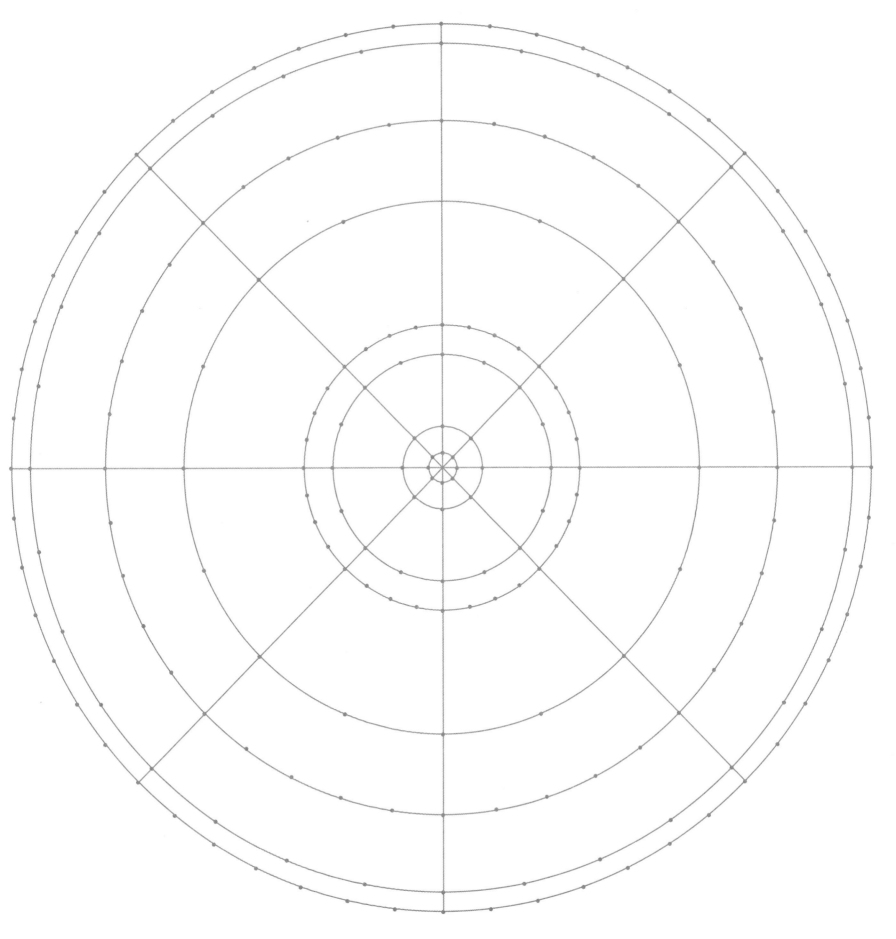

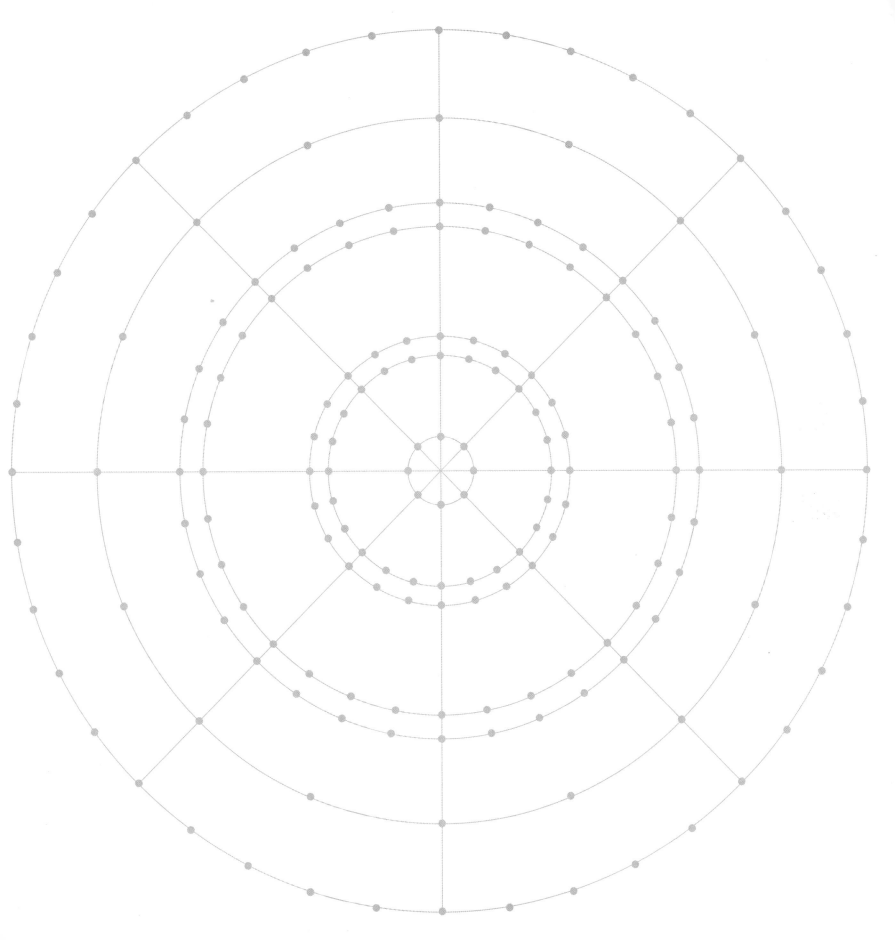

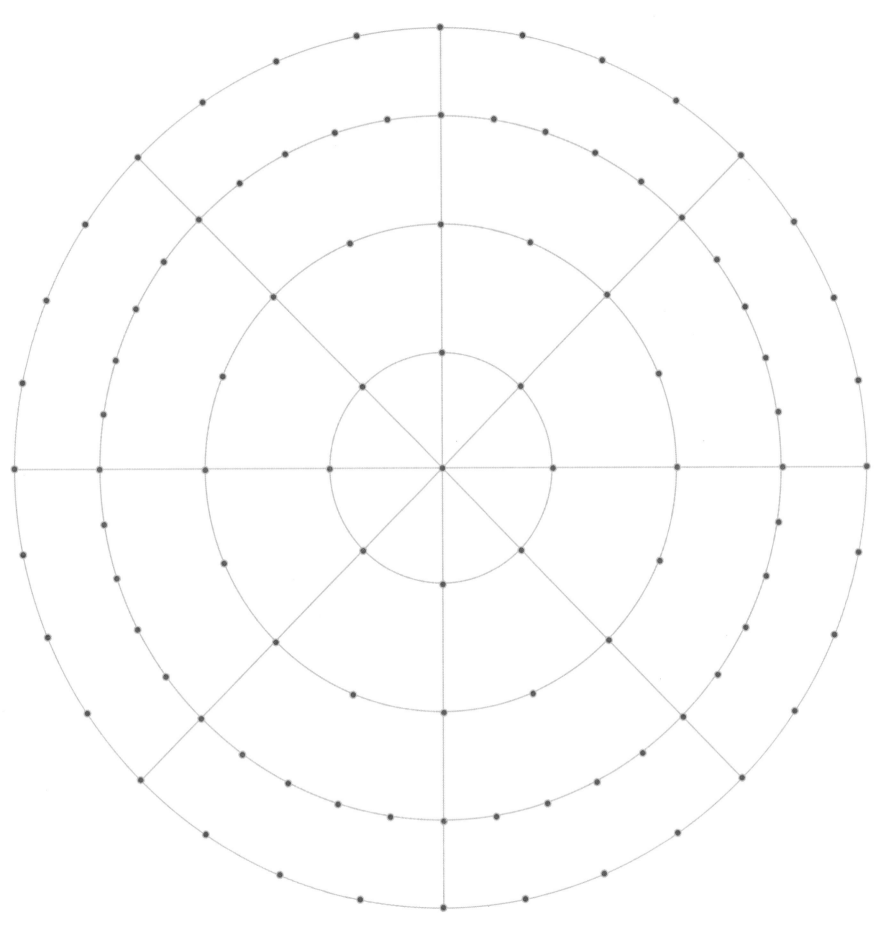

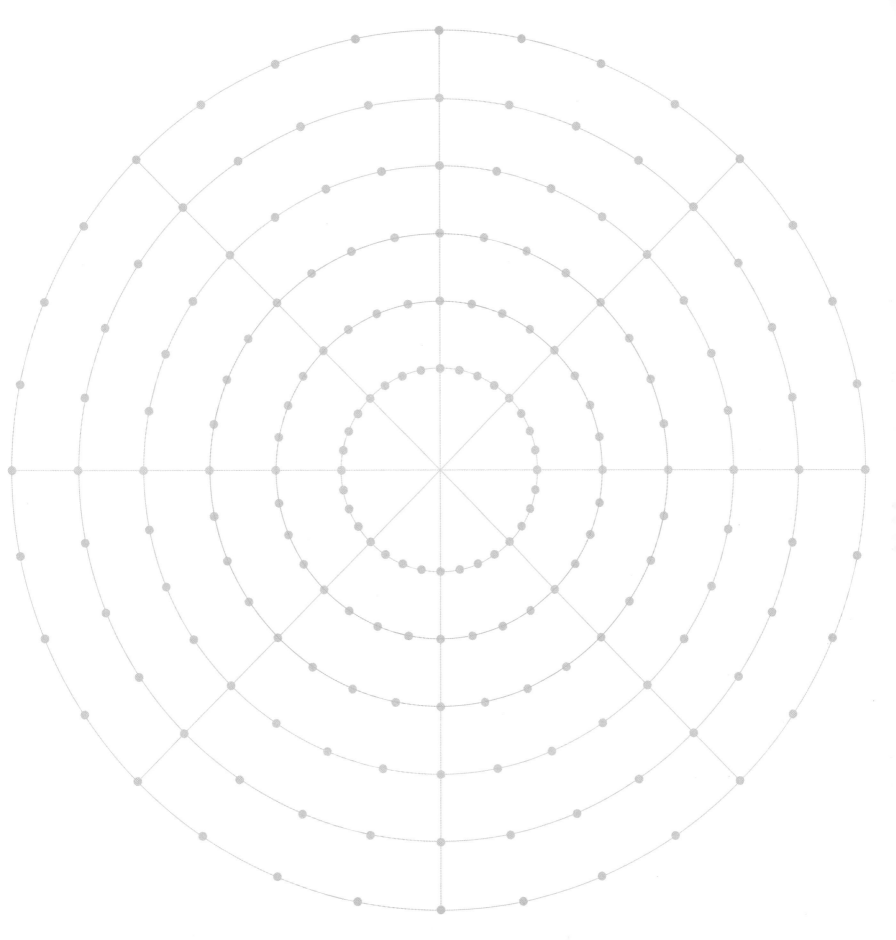

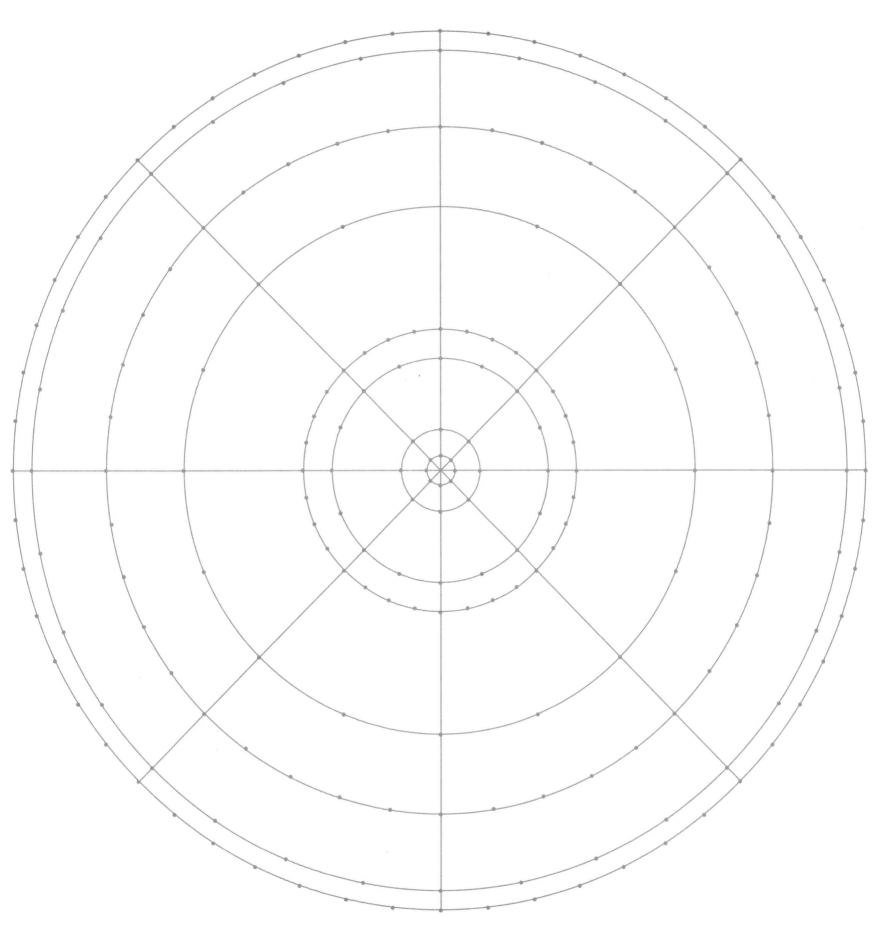

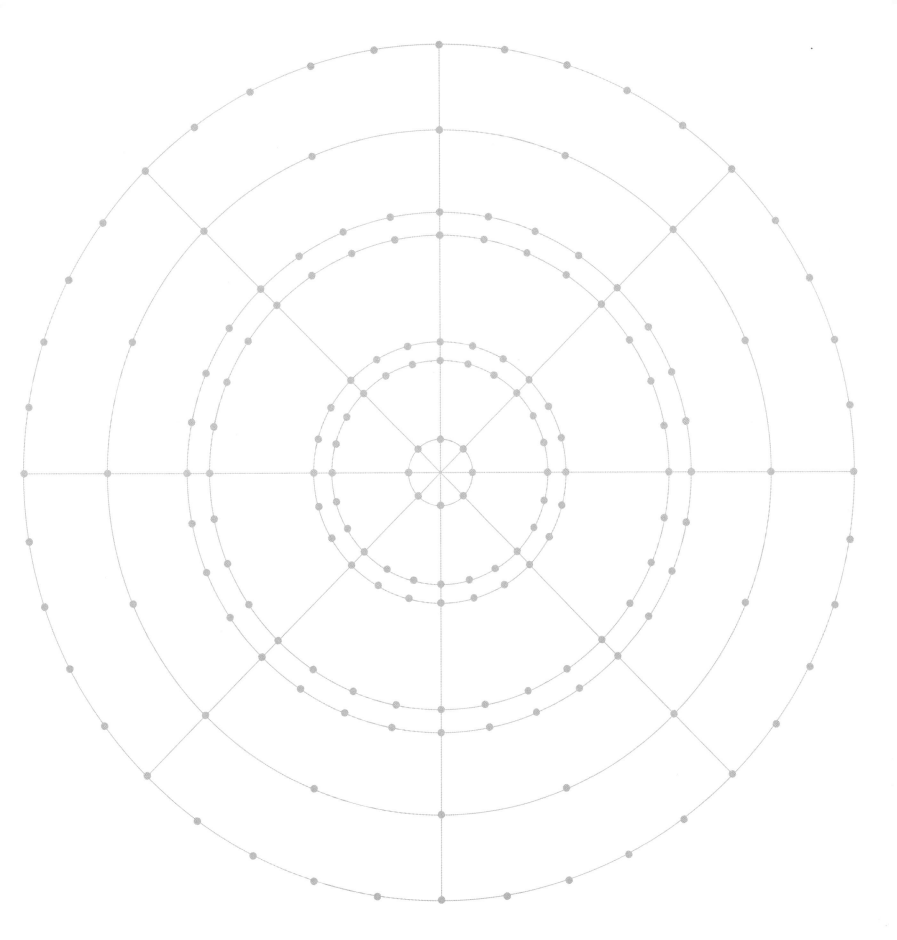

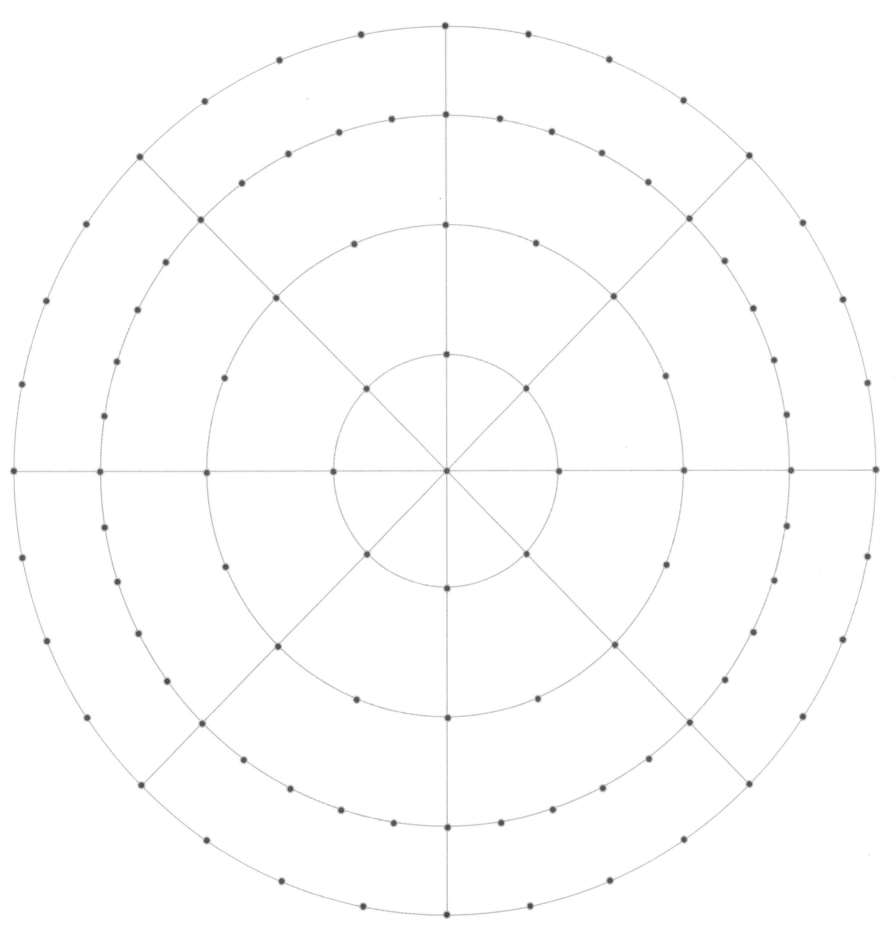

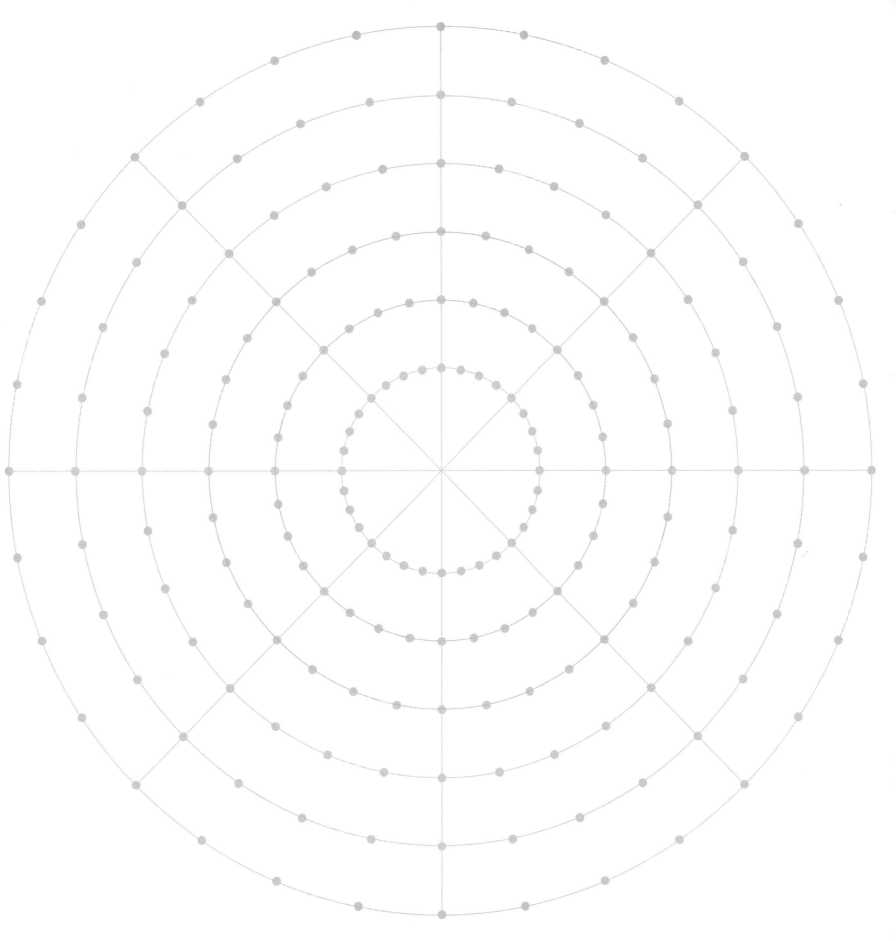

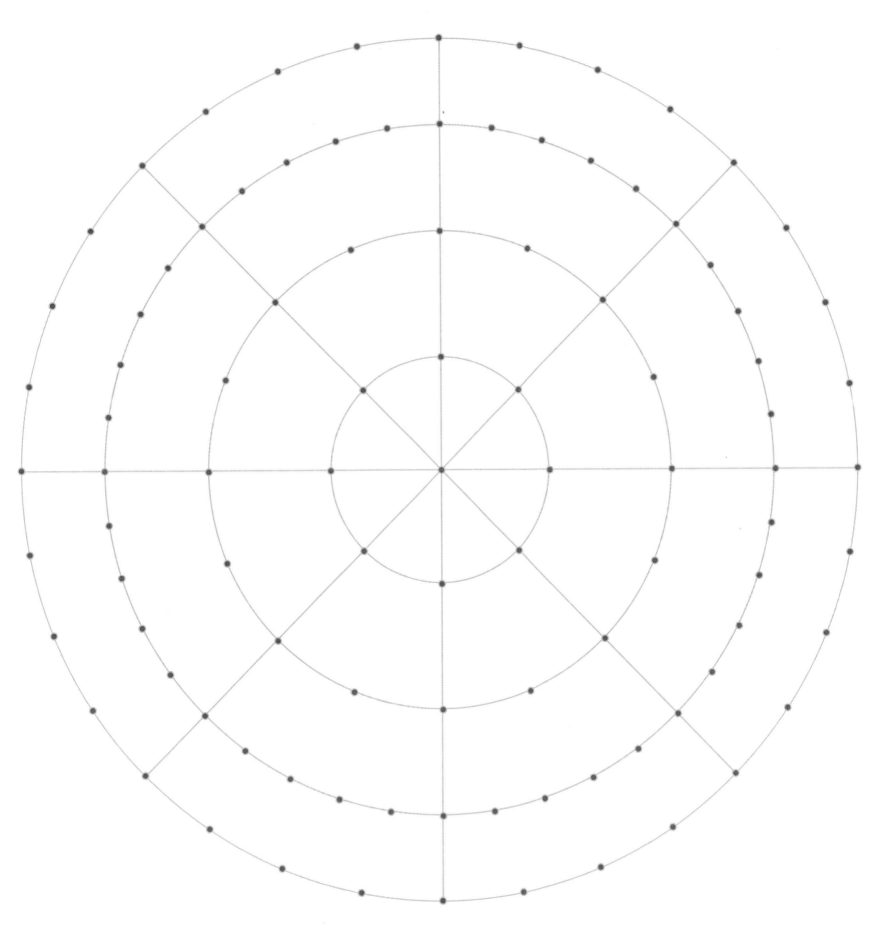

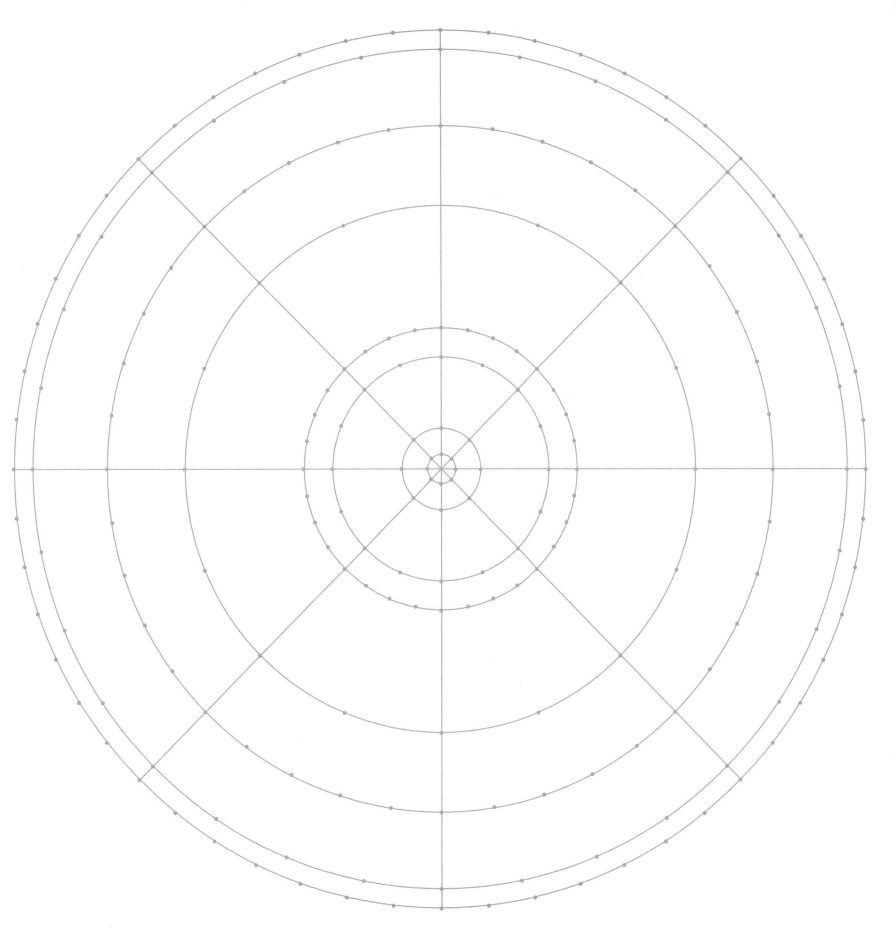

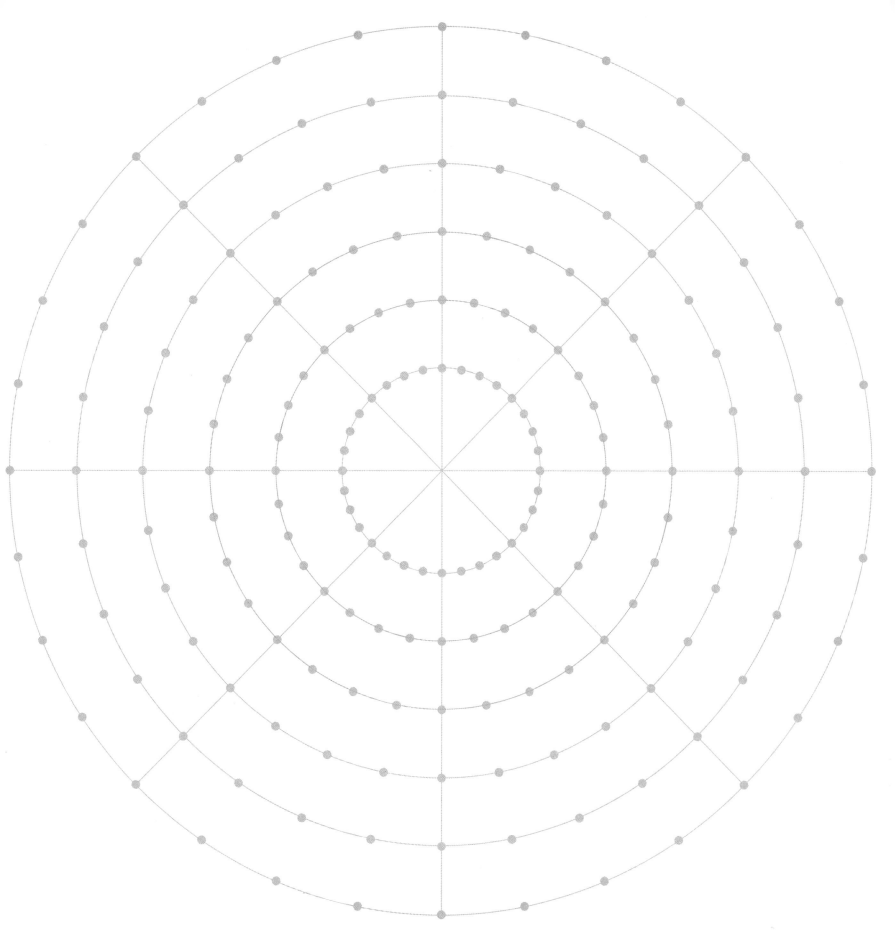

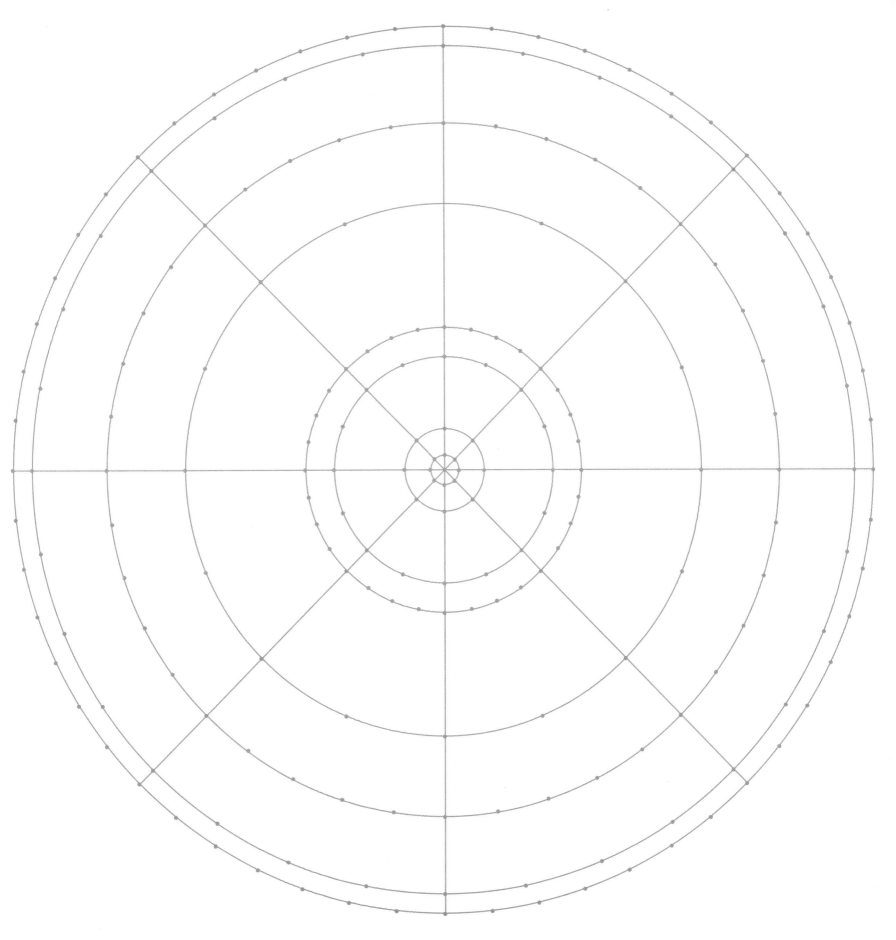

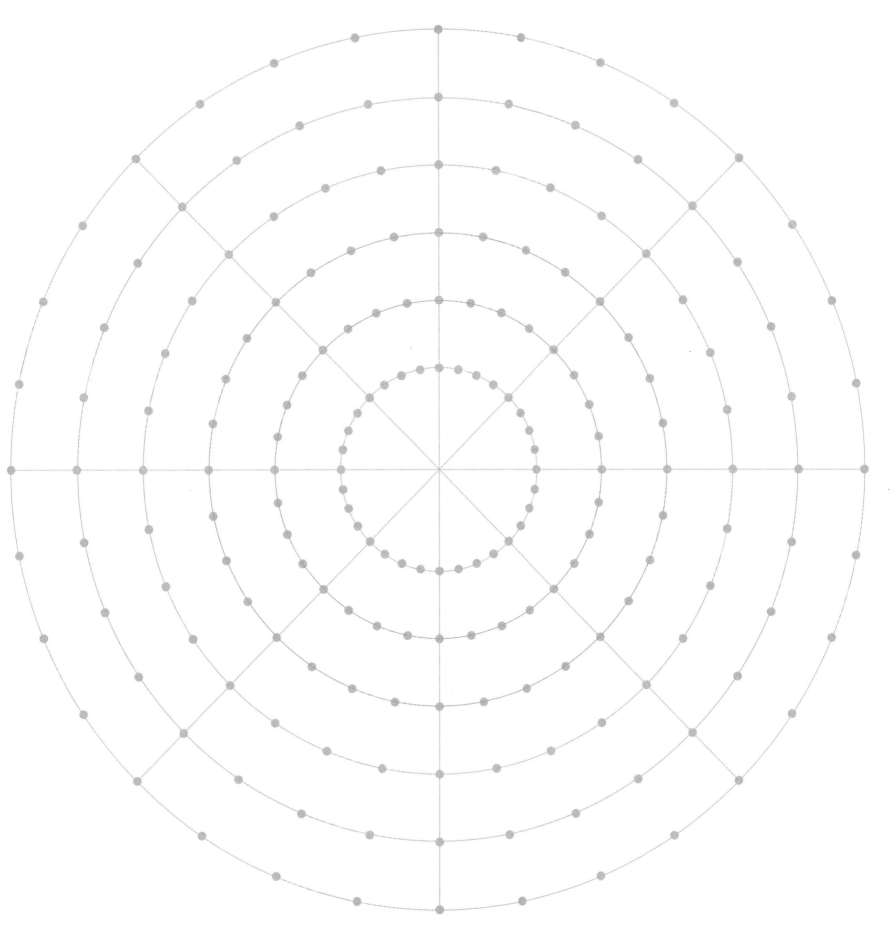

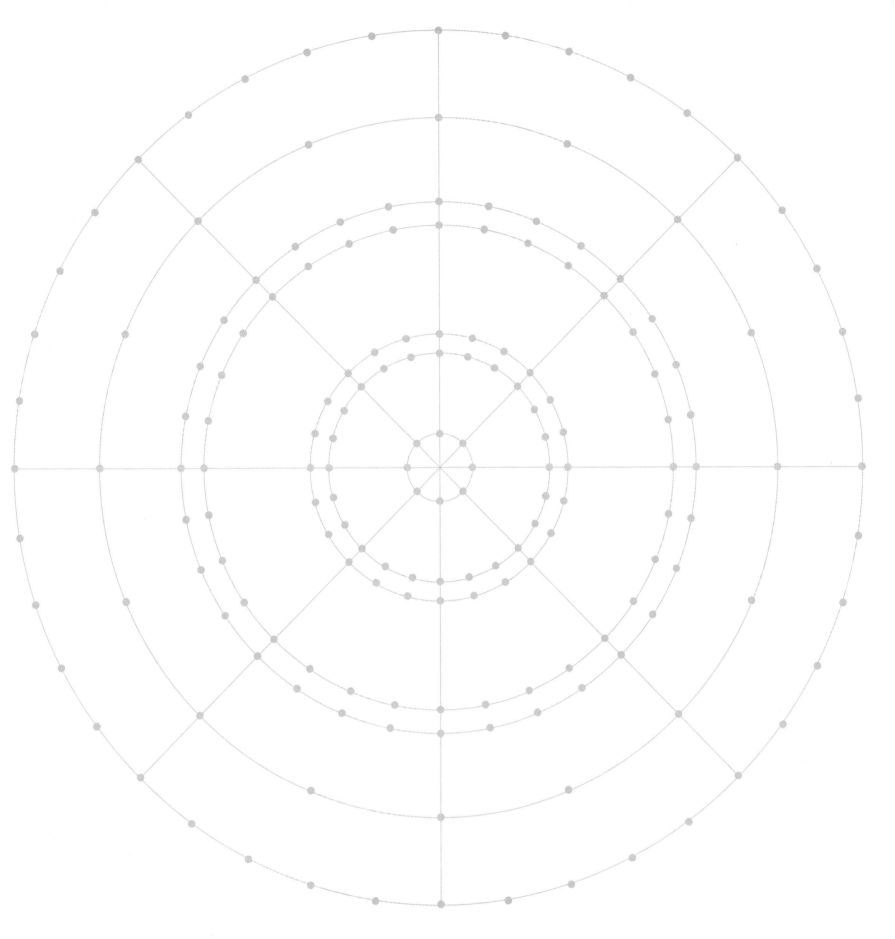

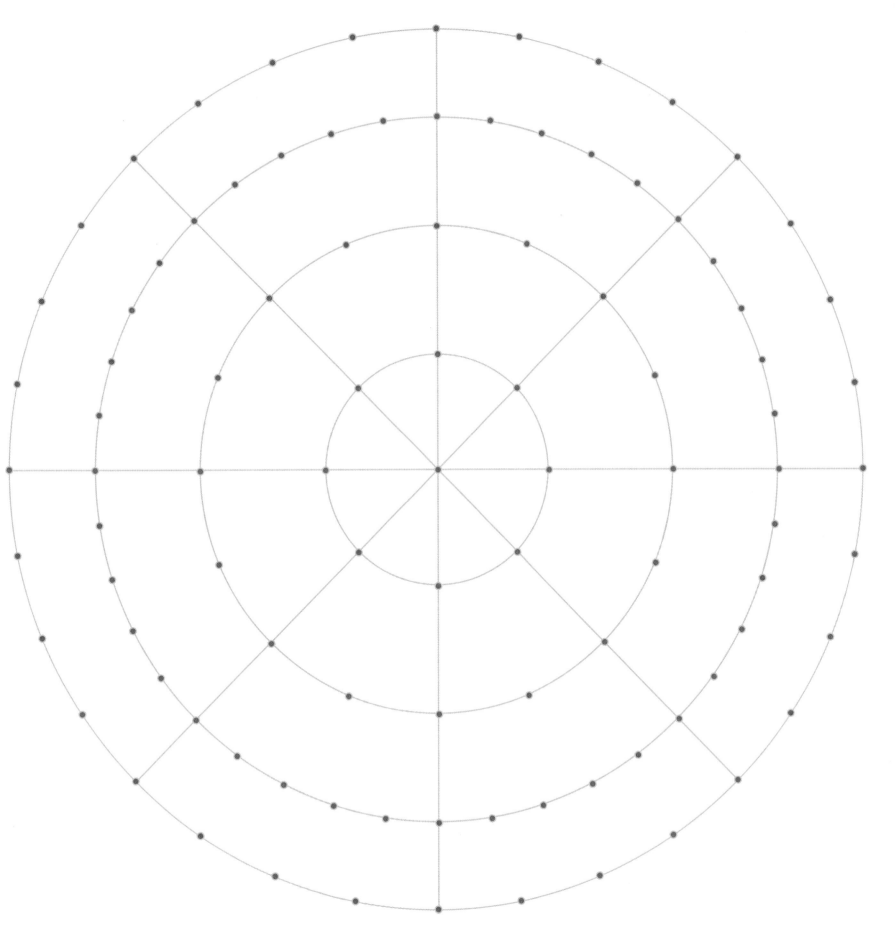

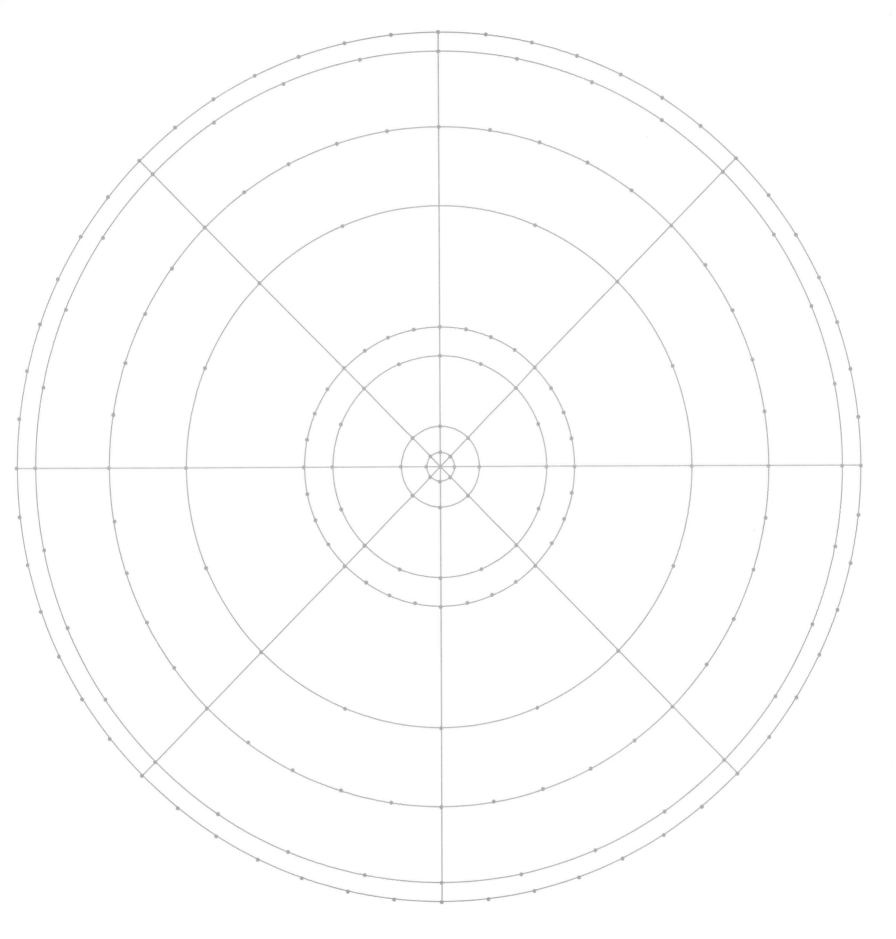

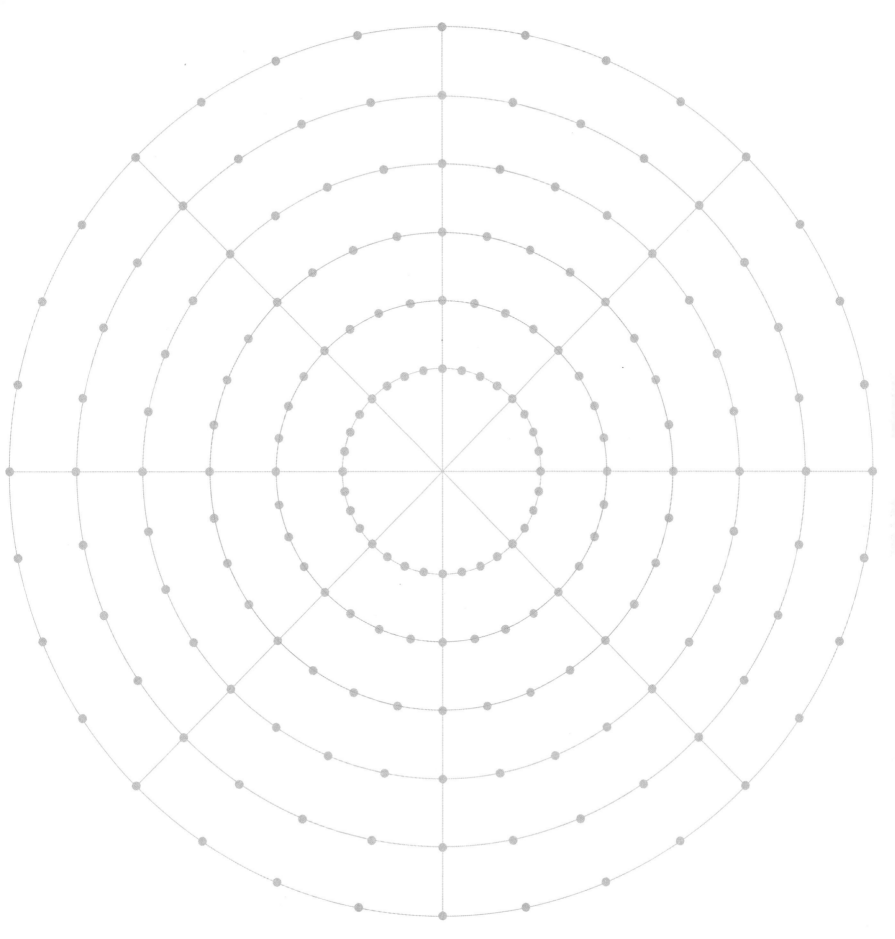

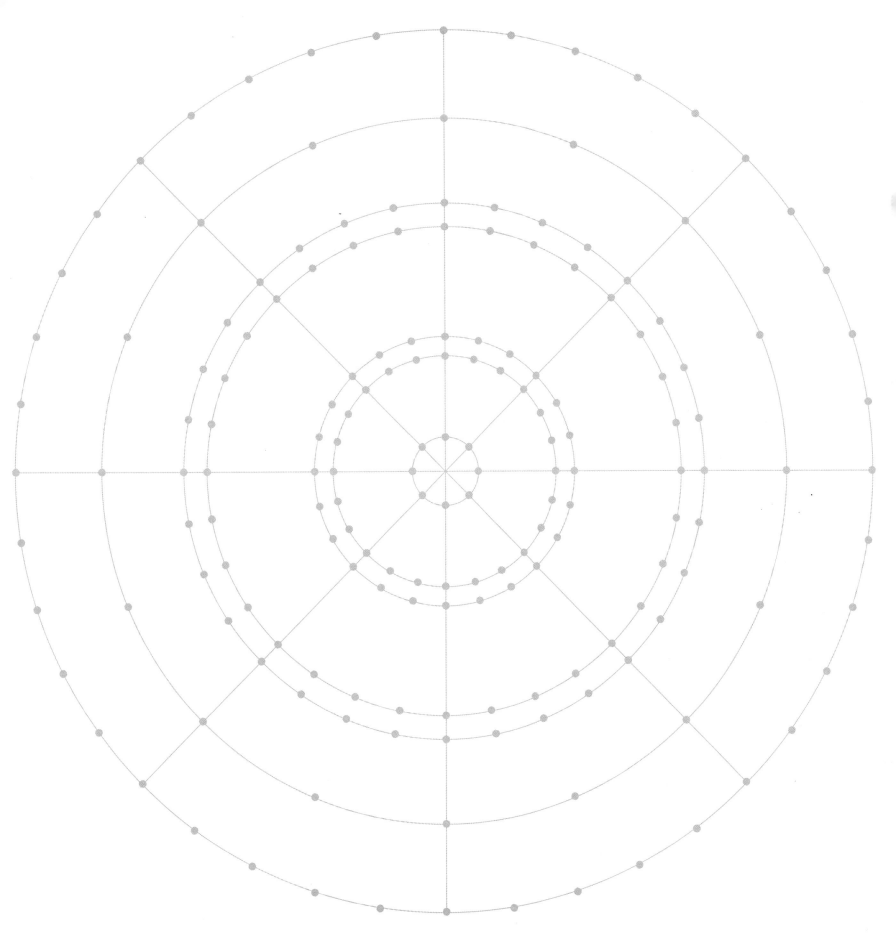

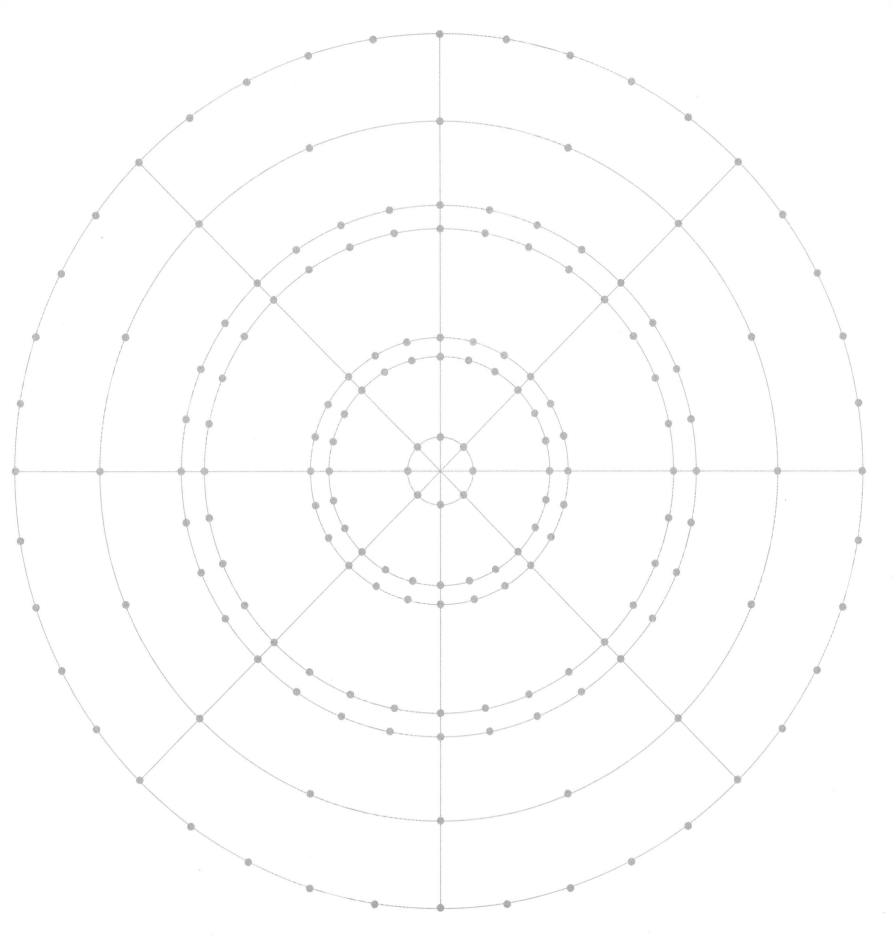

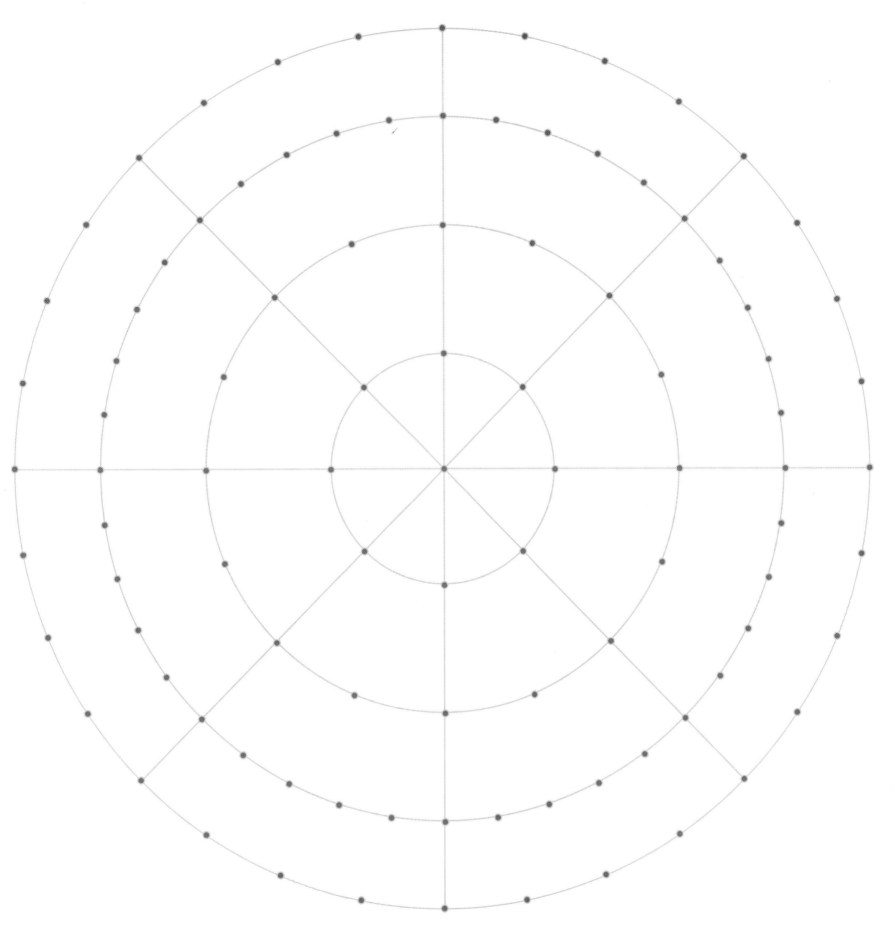

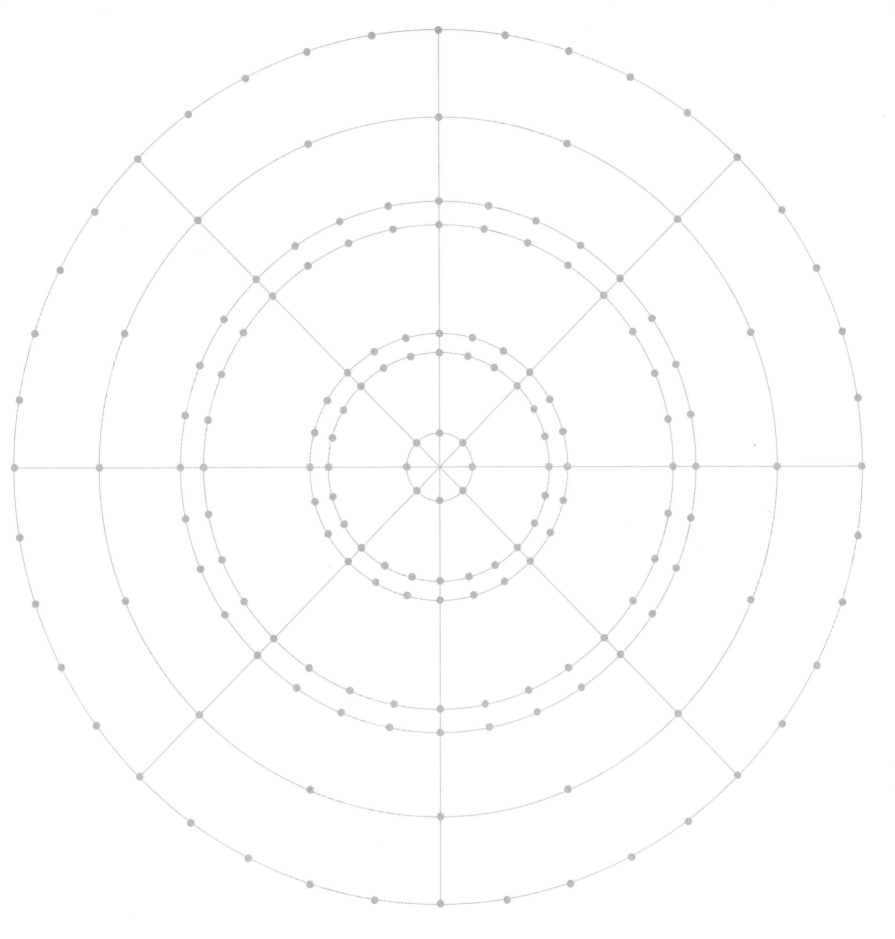

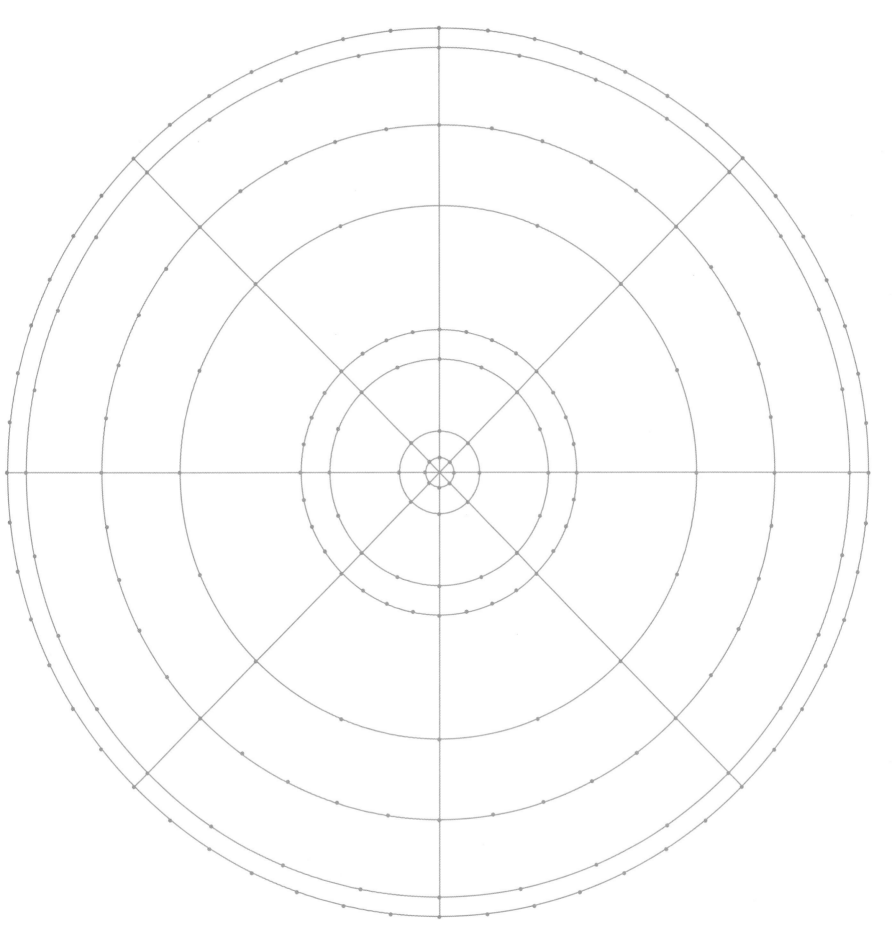

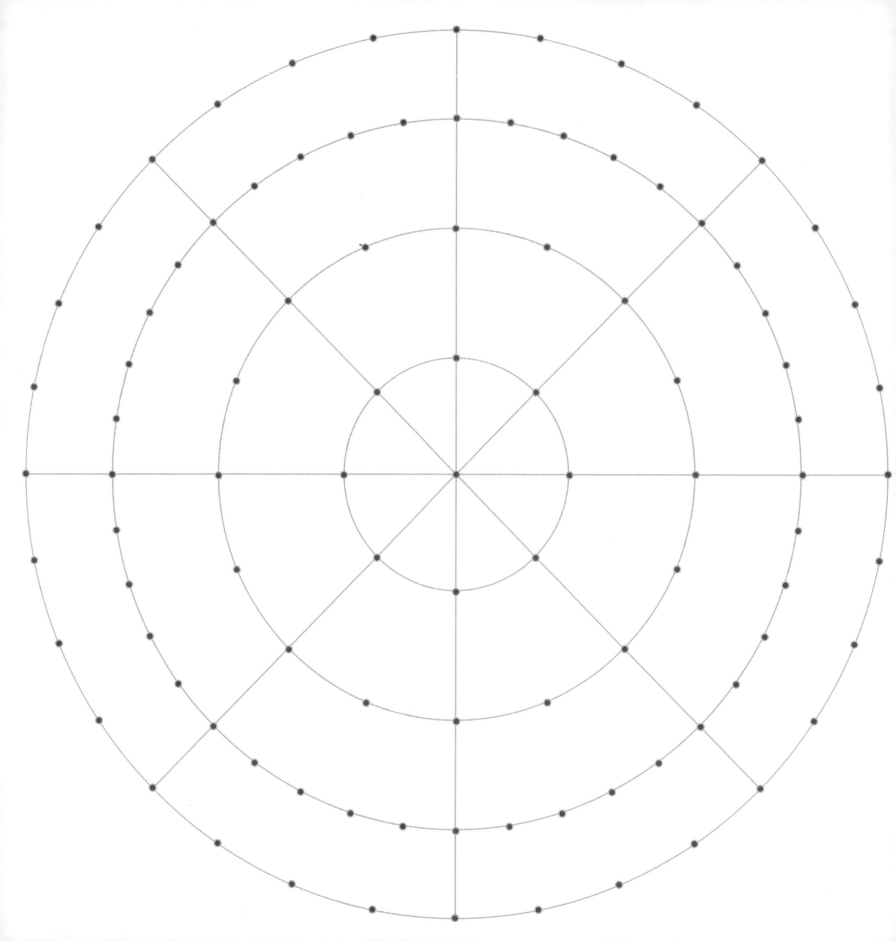

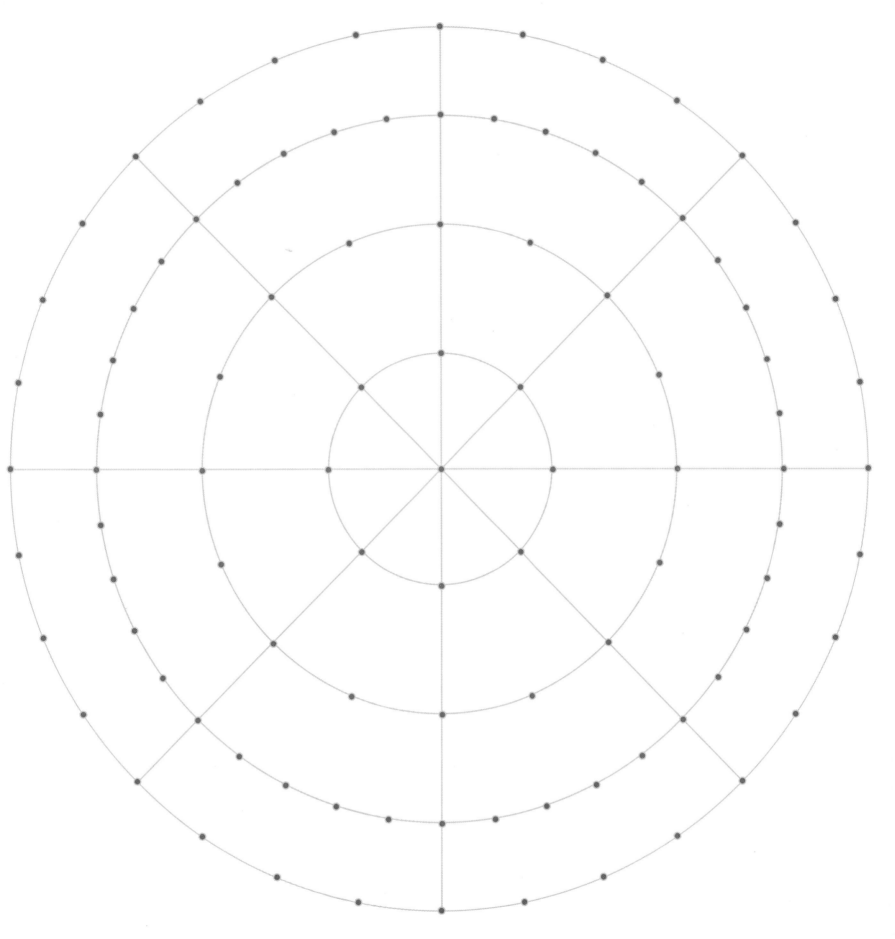

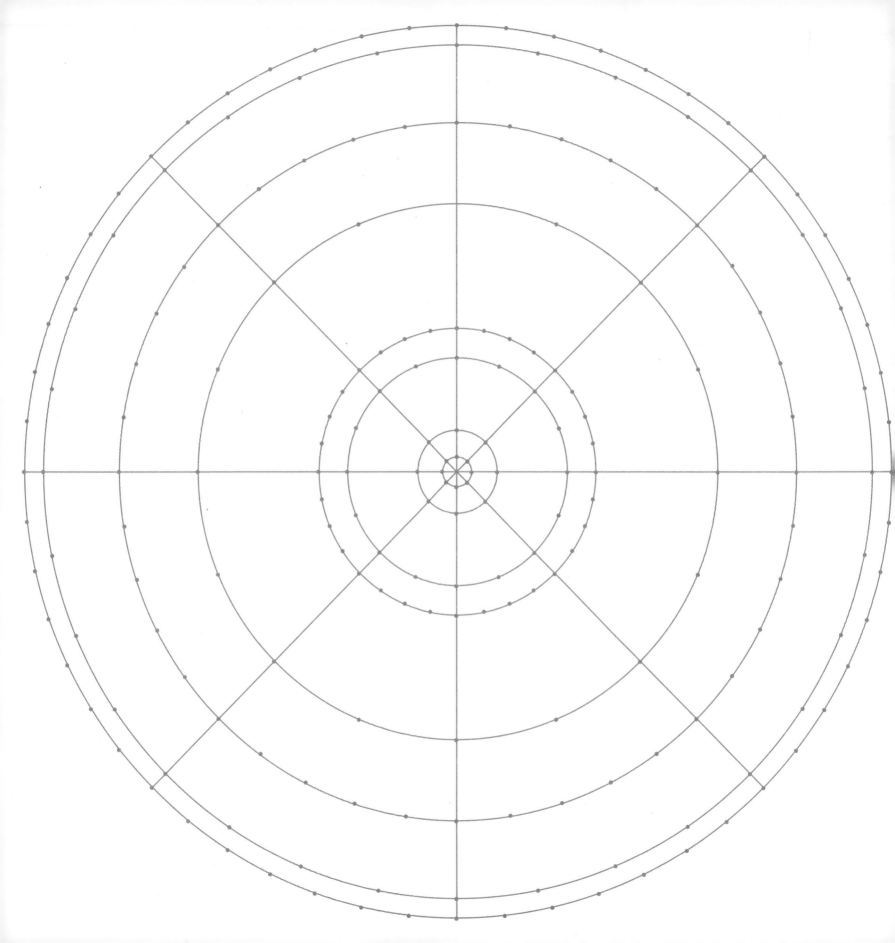

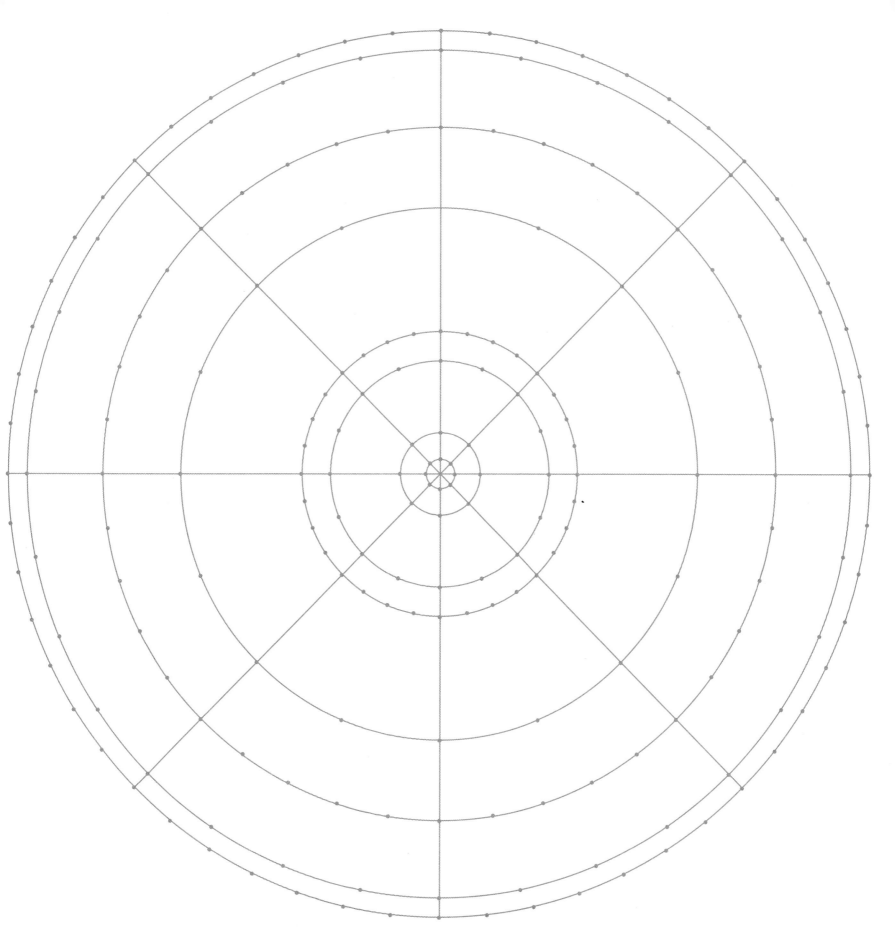

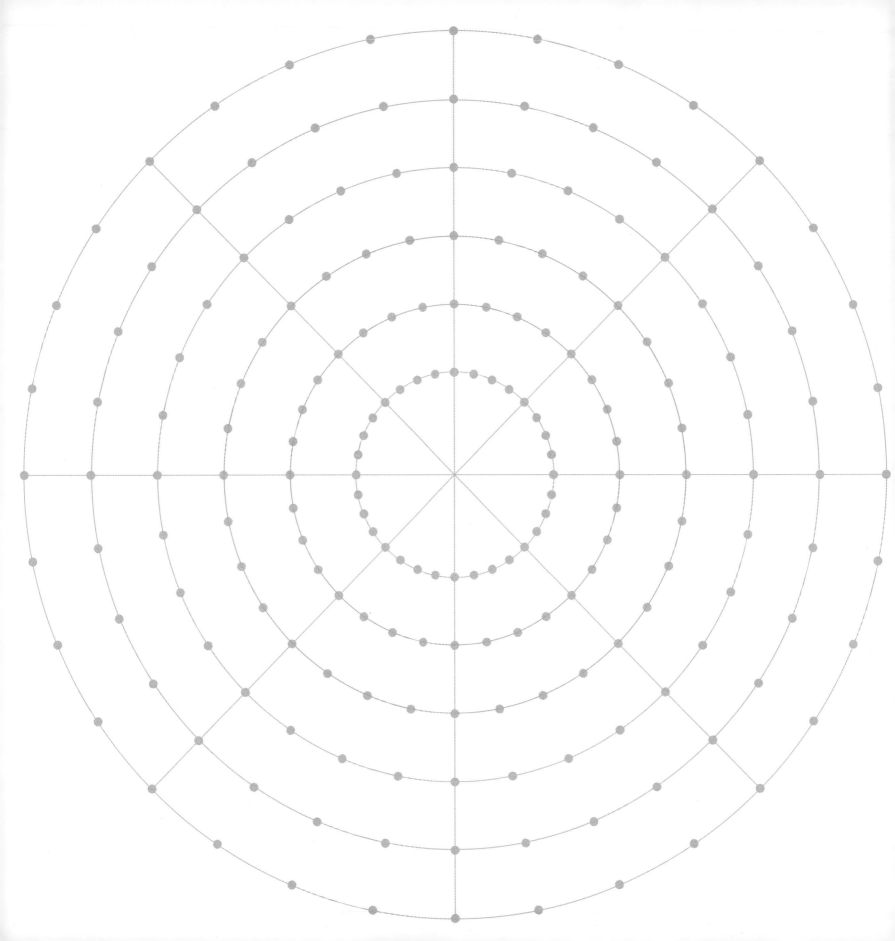

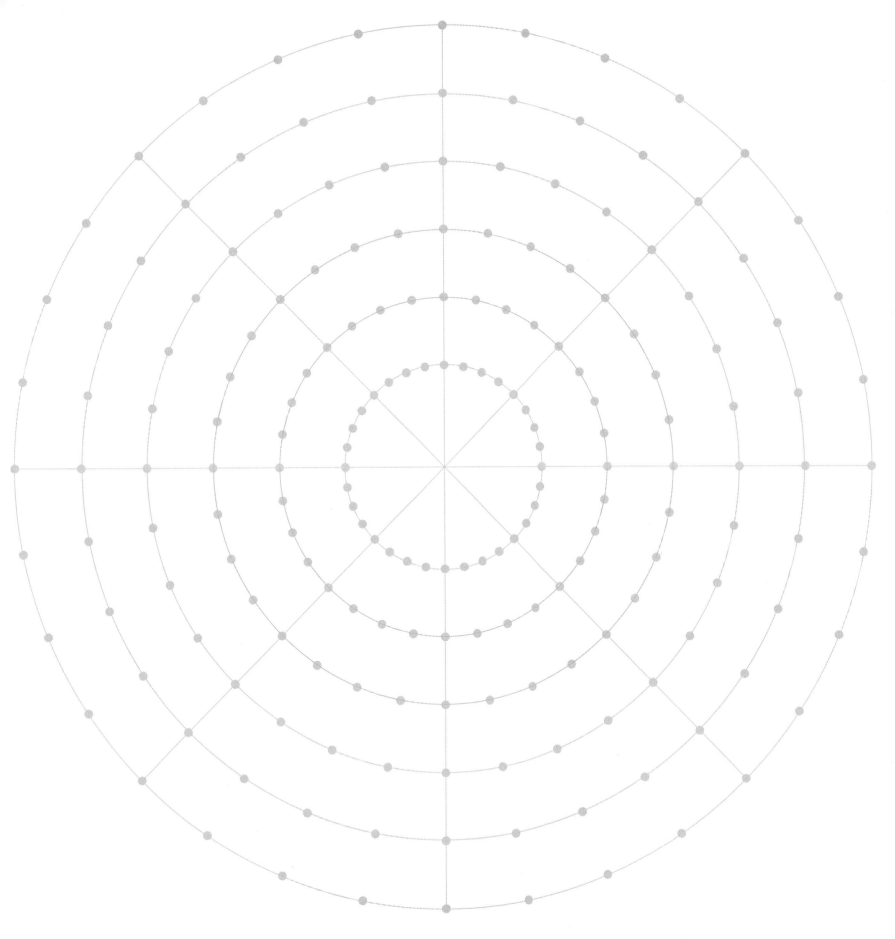

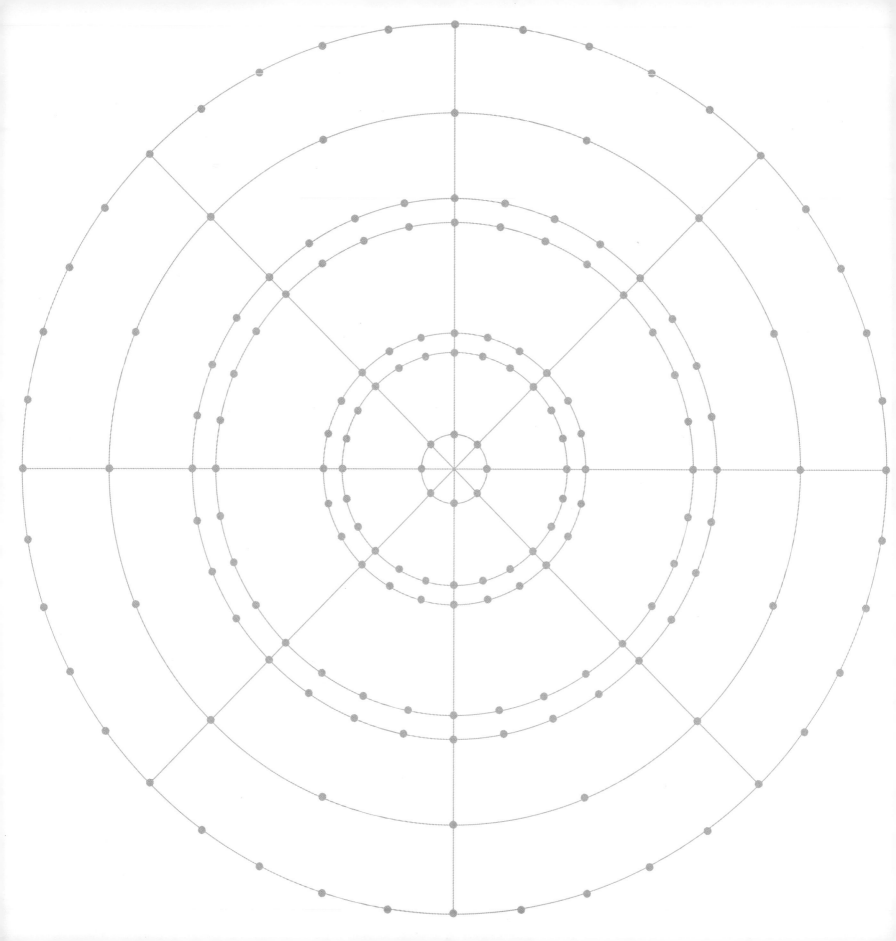

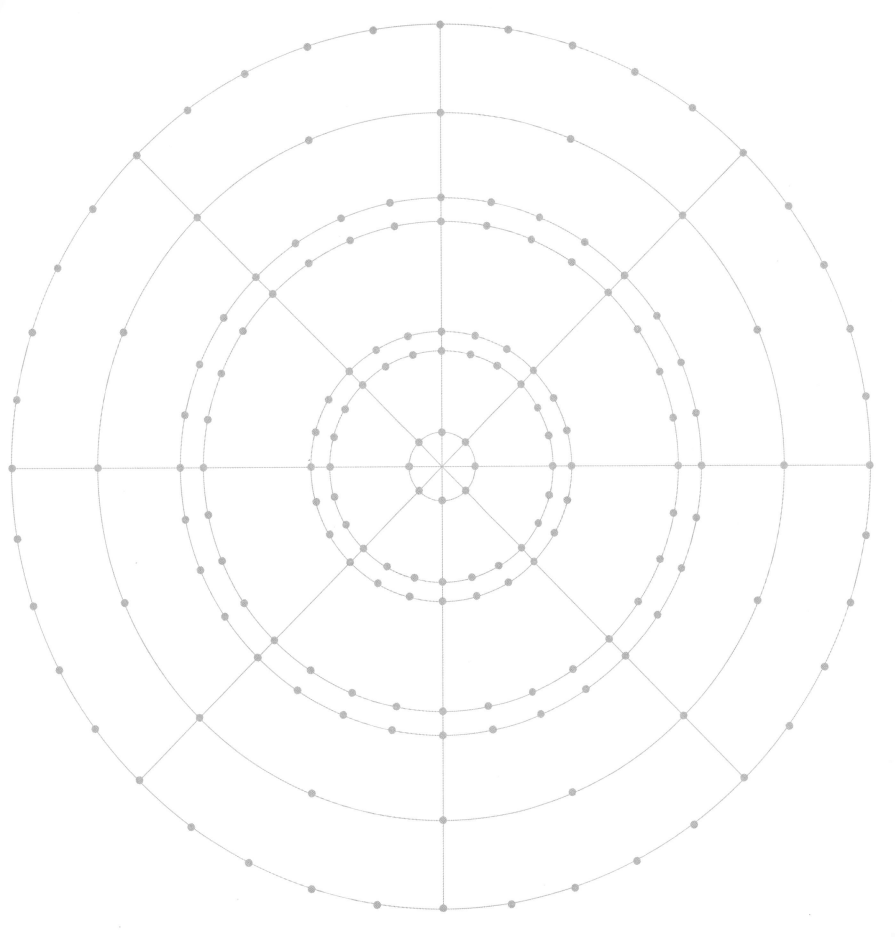

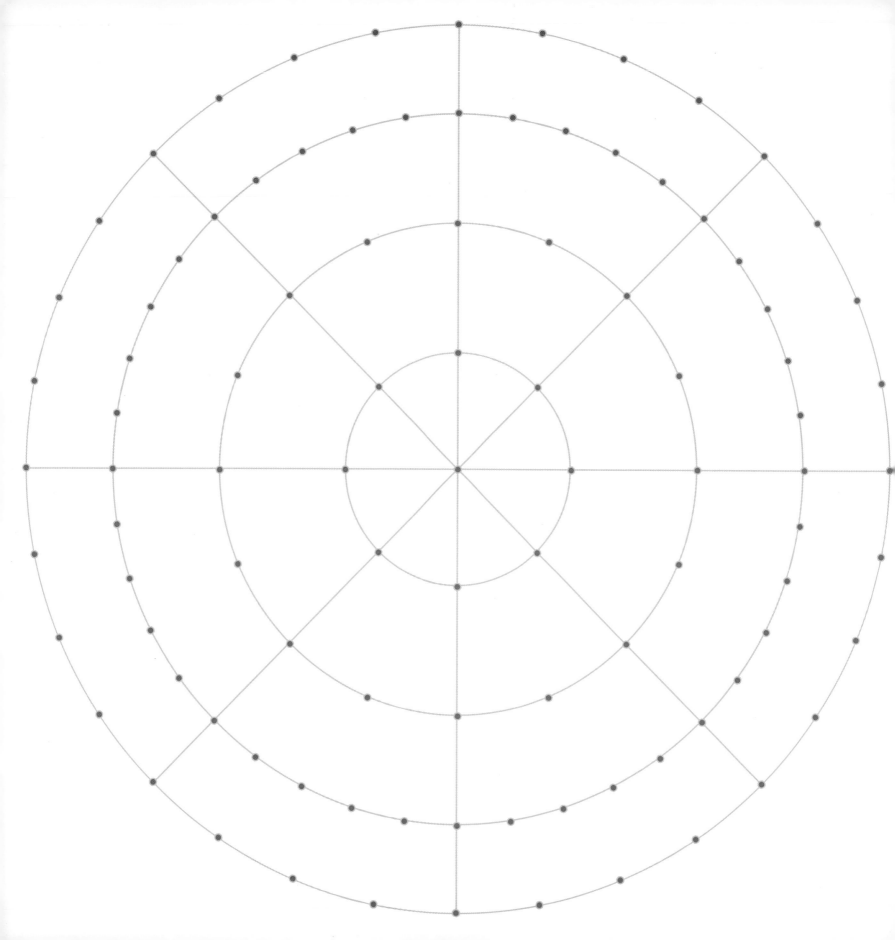

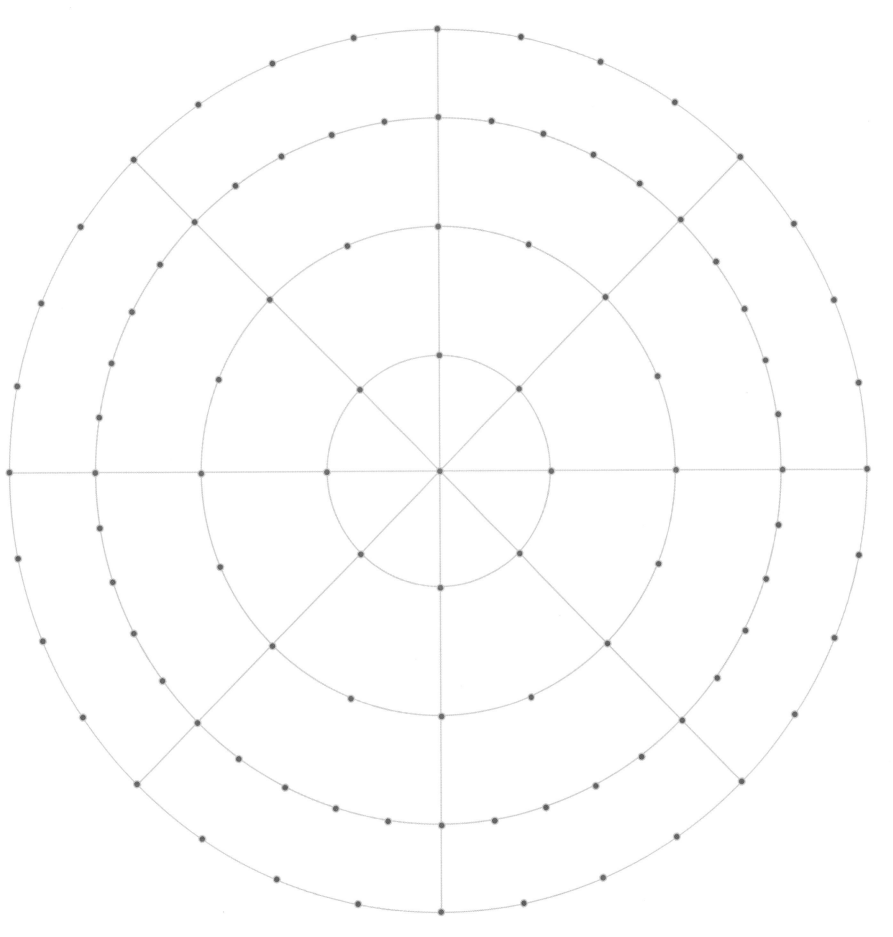

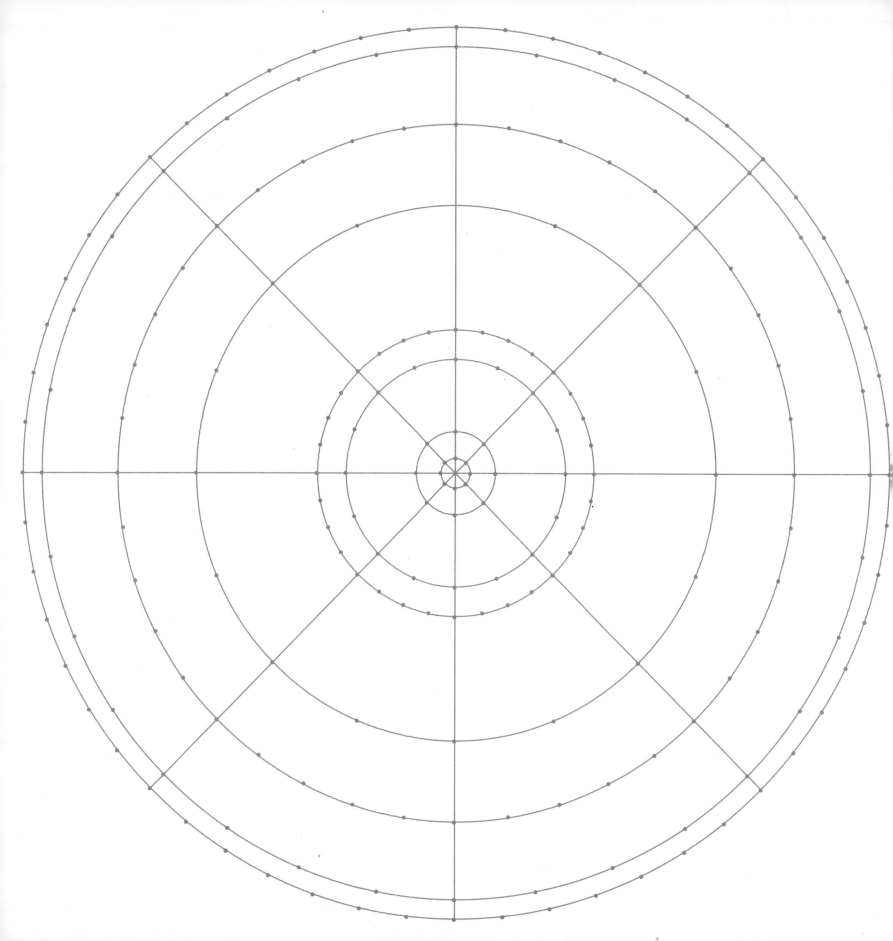

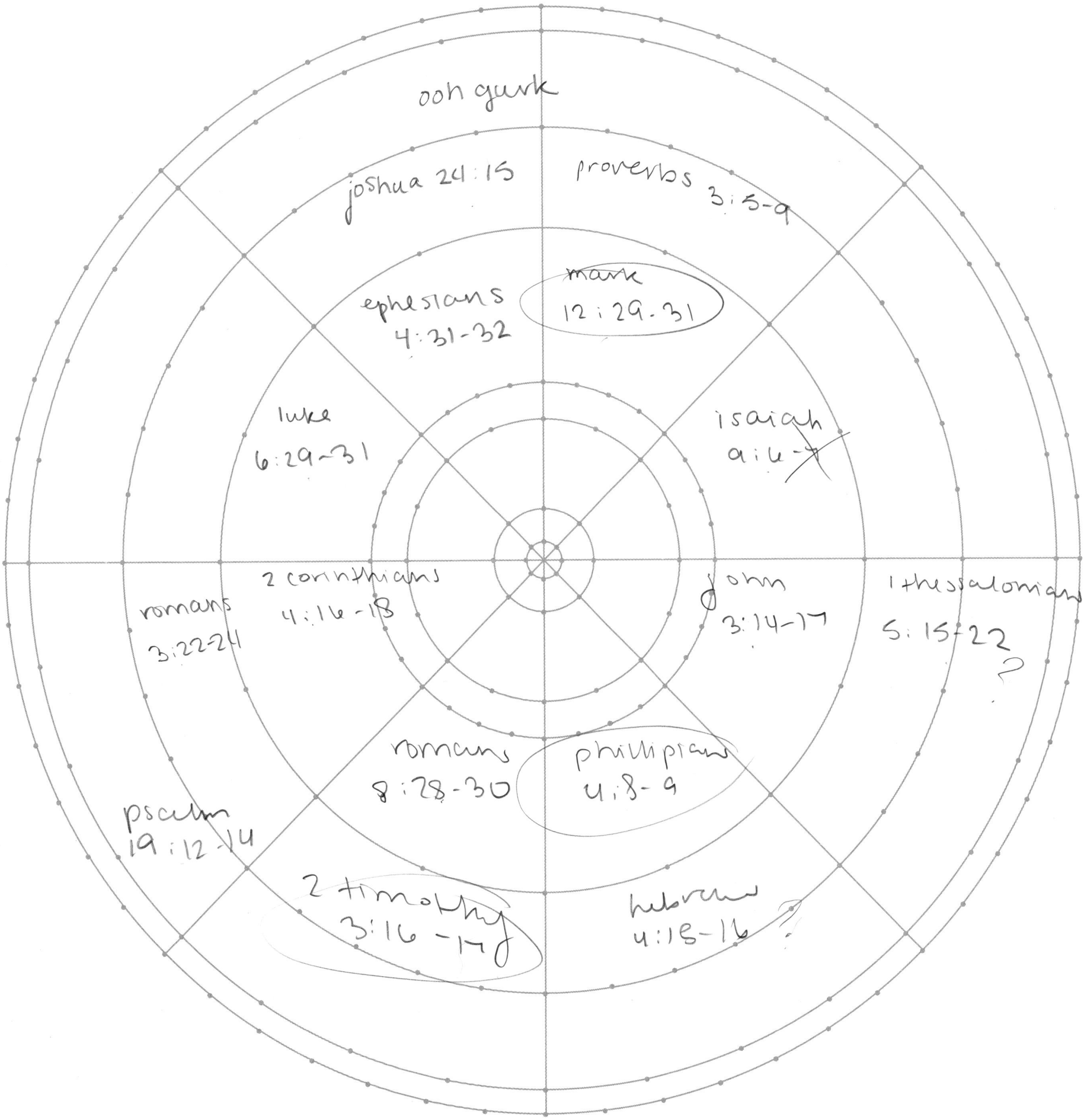

ooh gurk

joshua 24:15

proverbs 3:5-9

ephesians
4:31-32

mark
12:29-31

luke
6:29-31

isaiah
41:6-7

2 corinthians
4:16-18

romans
3:22-24

john
3:14-17

1 thessalonians
5:15-22
?

romans
8:28-30

phillipians
4:8-9

psalm
19:12-14

2 timothy
3:16-17

hebrews
4:15-16 ?

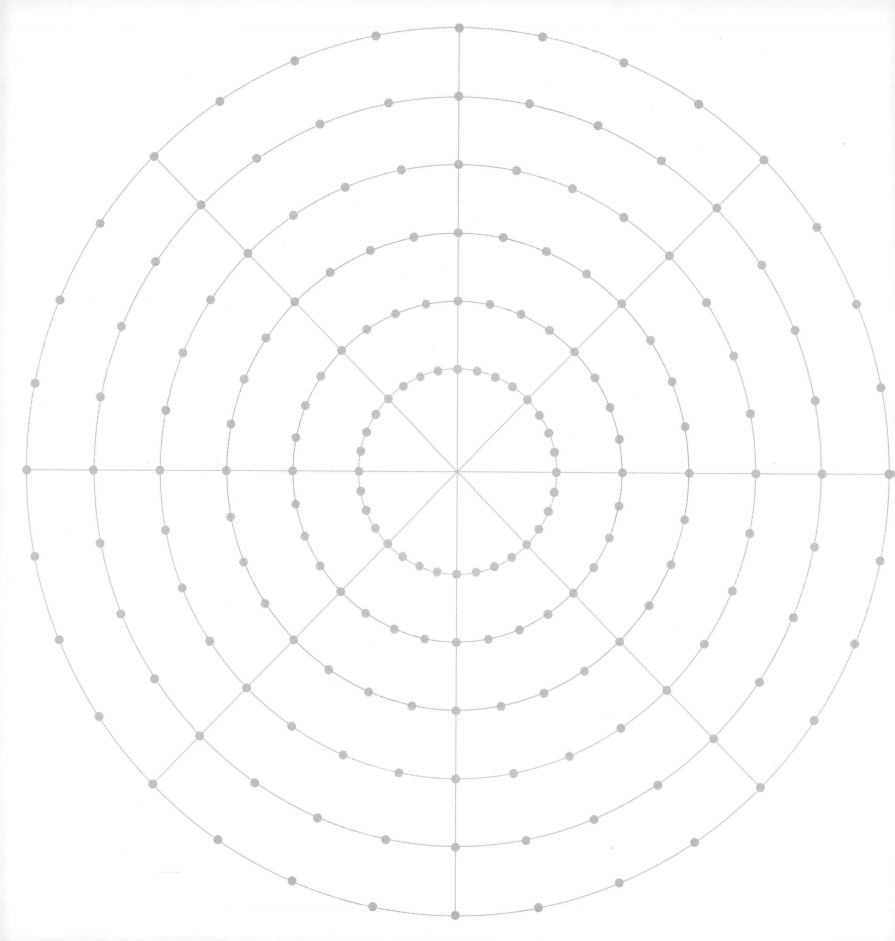

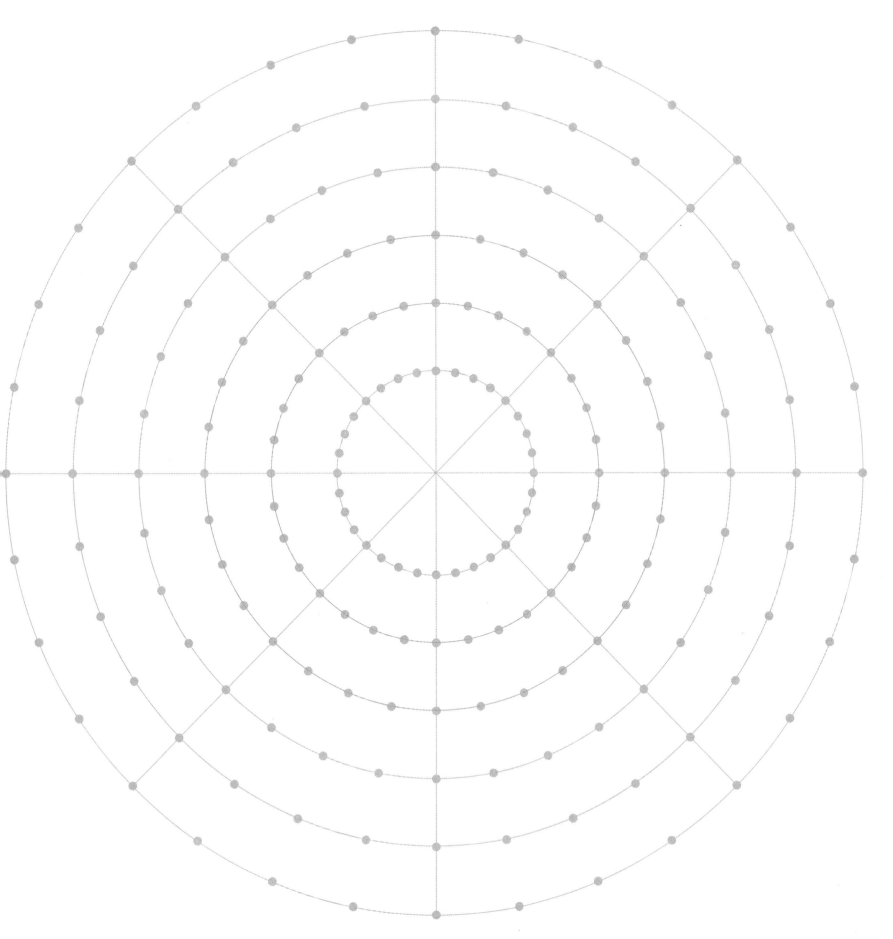

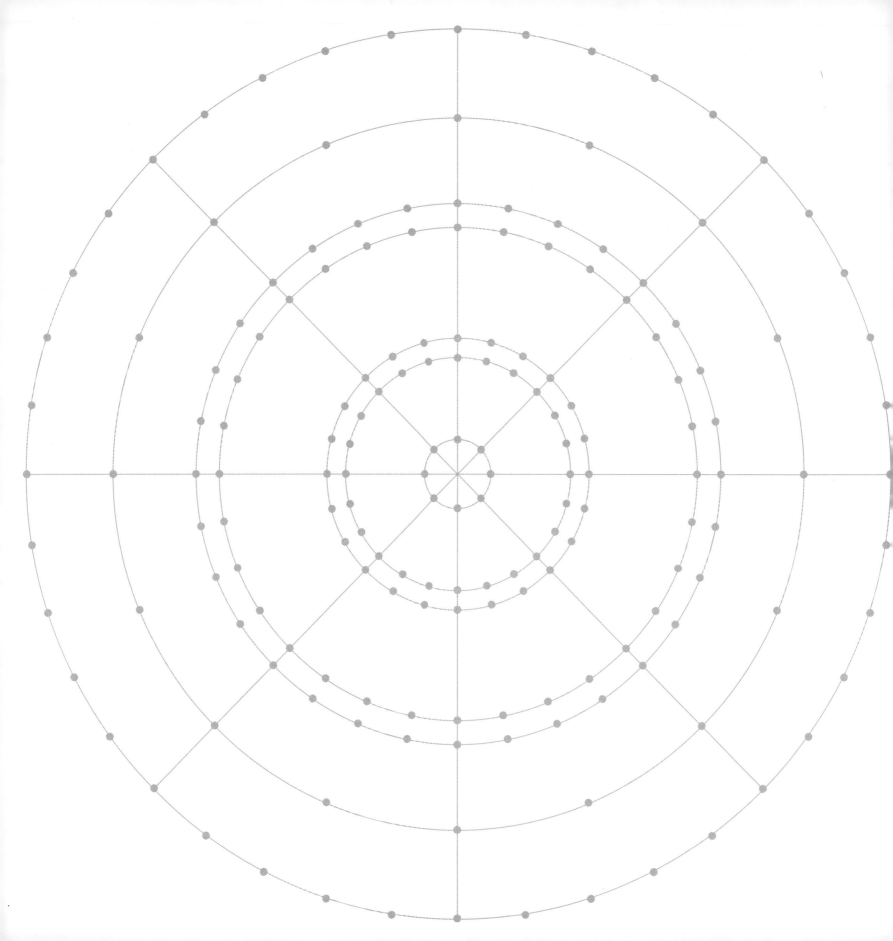

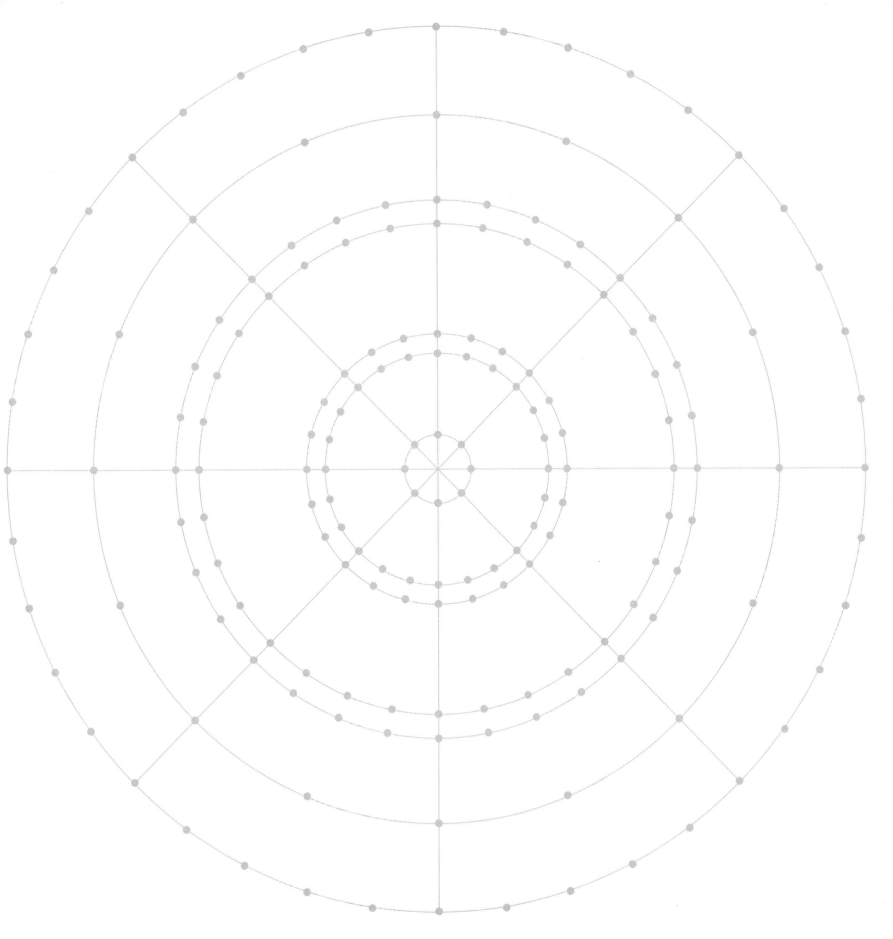

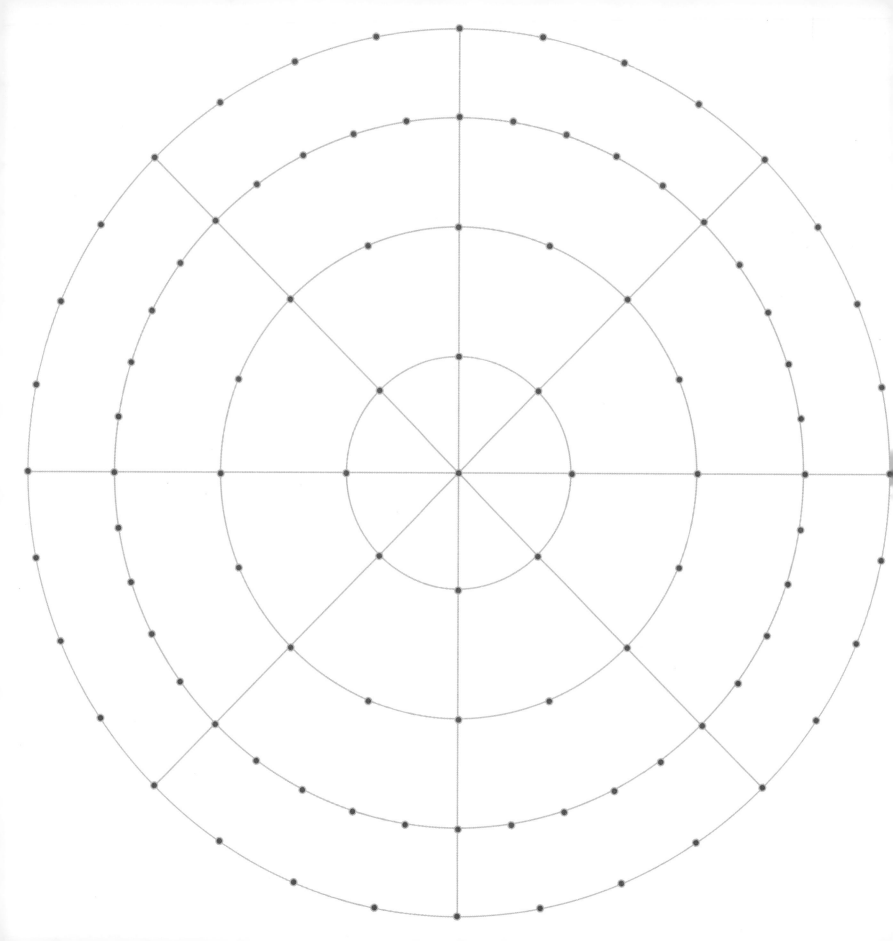

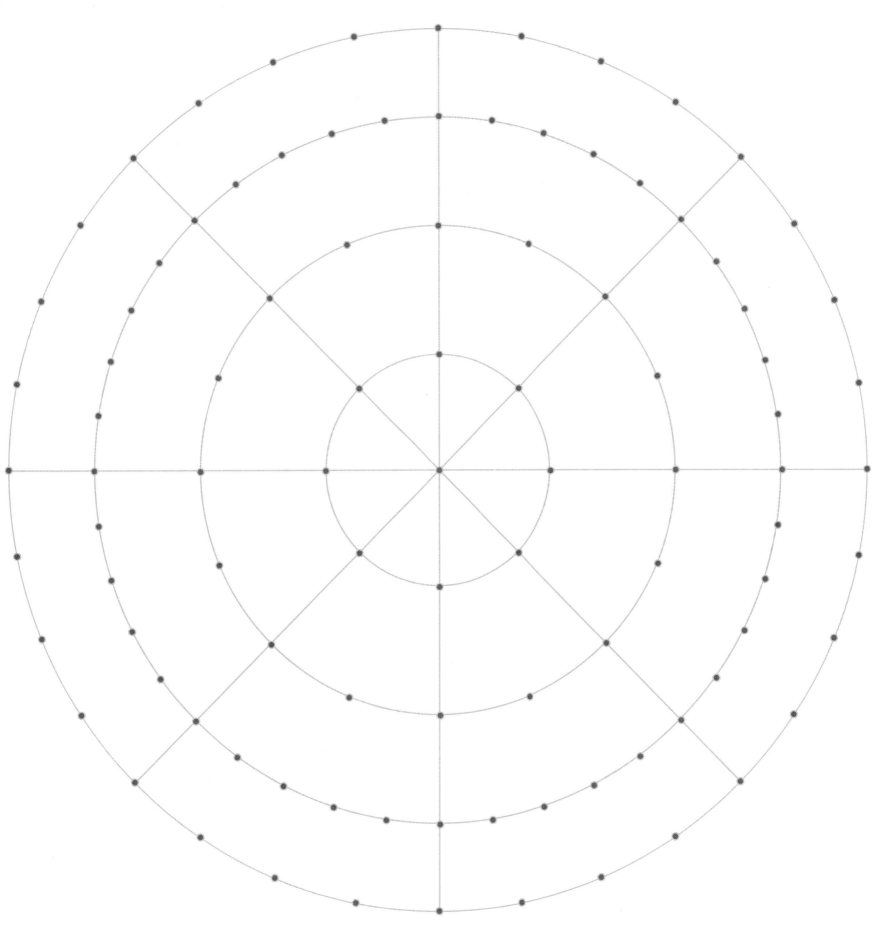

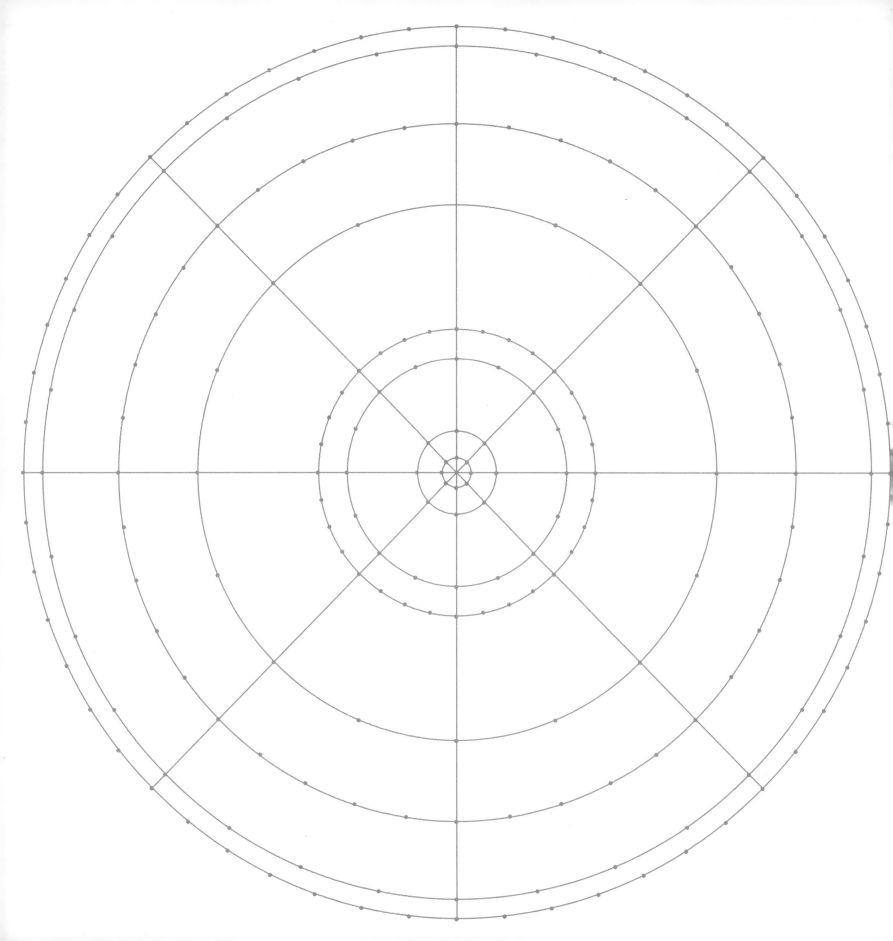

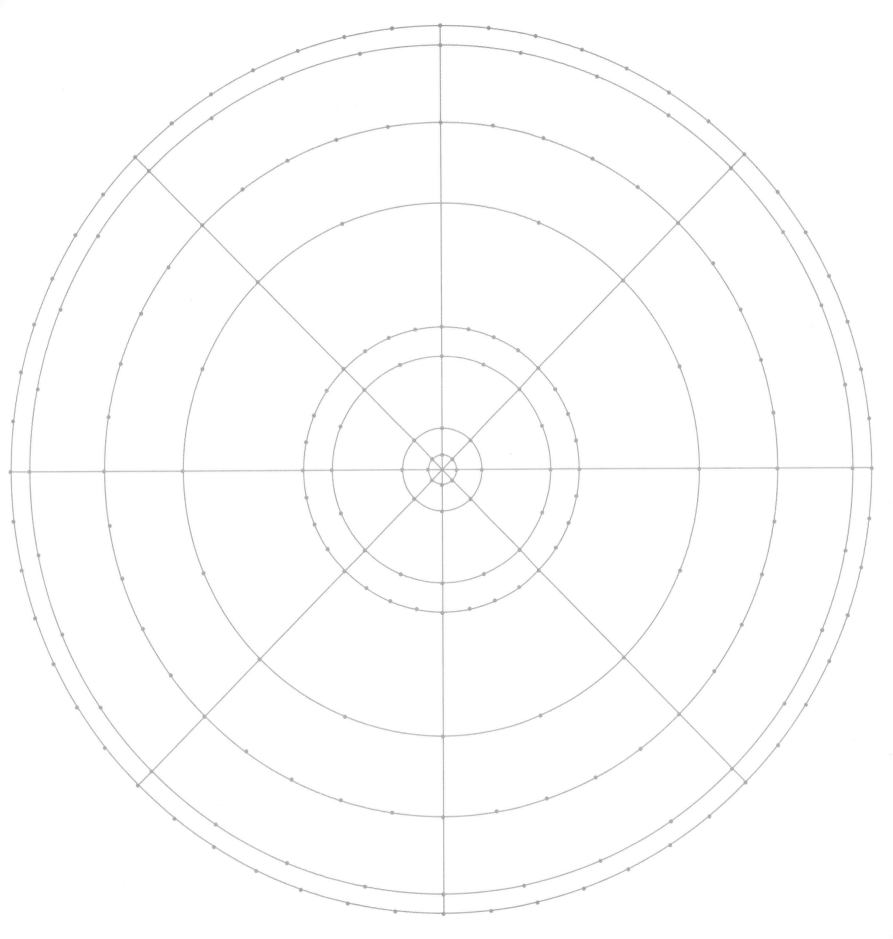

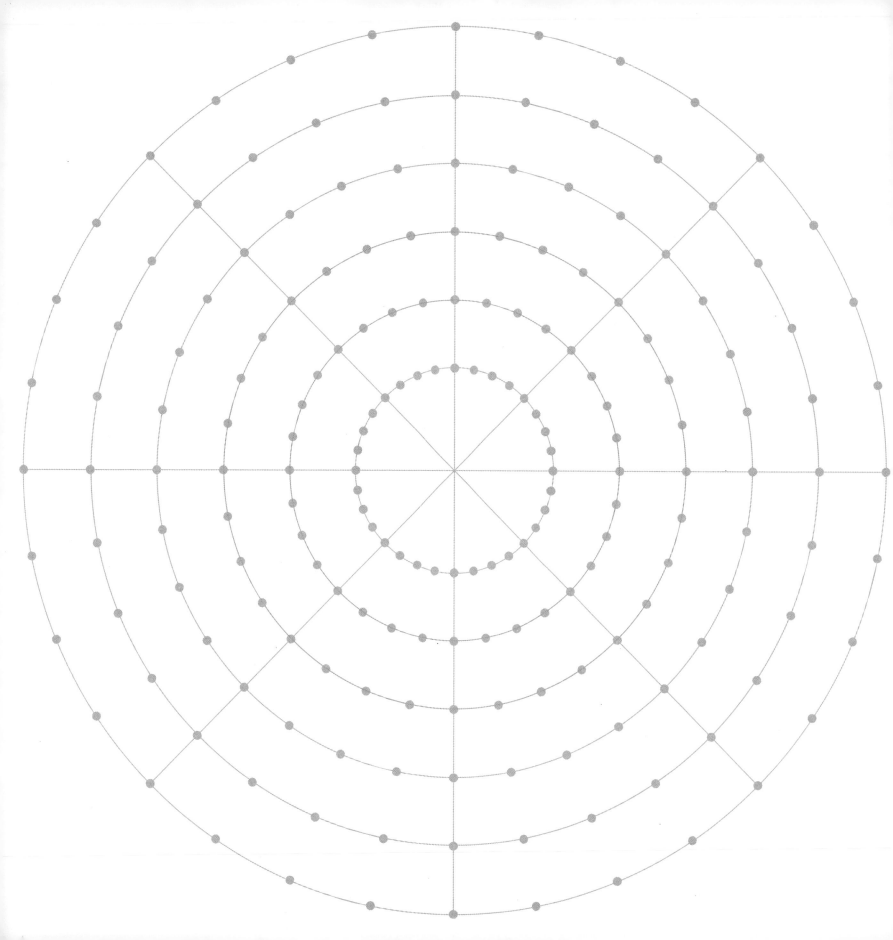

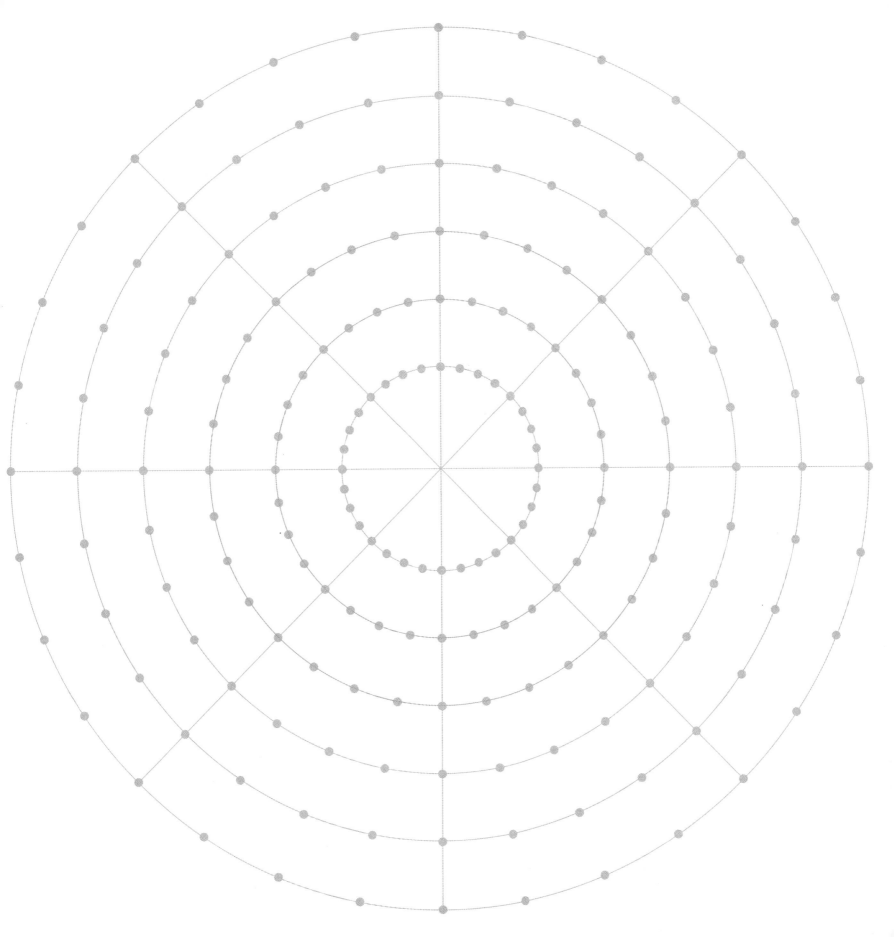

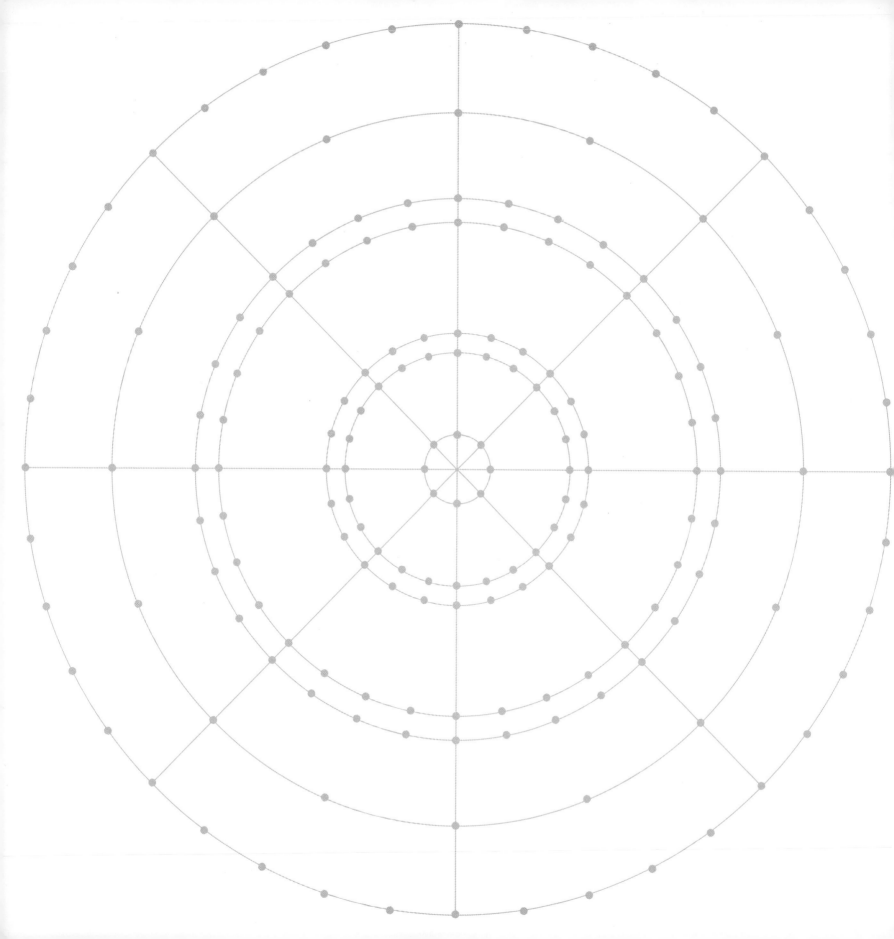

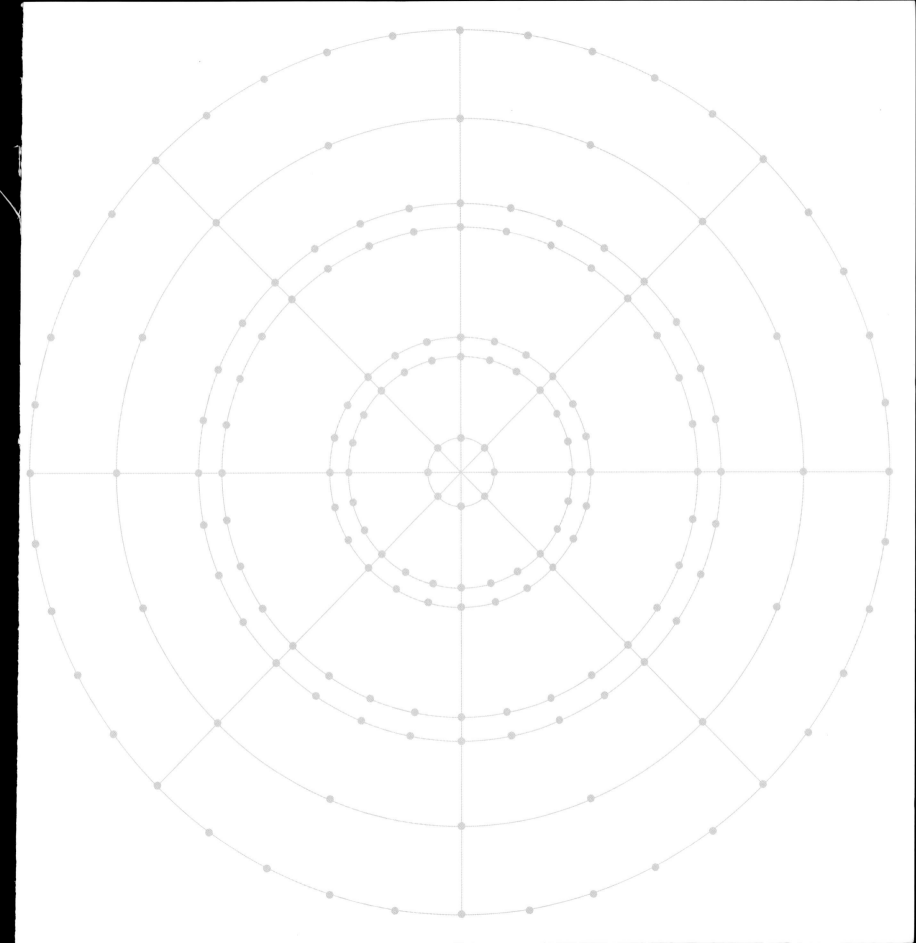

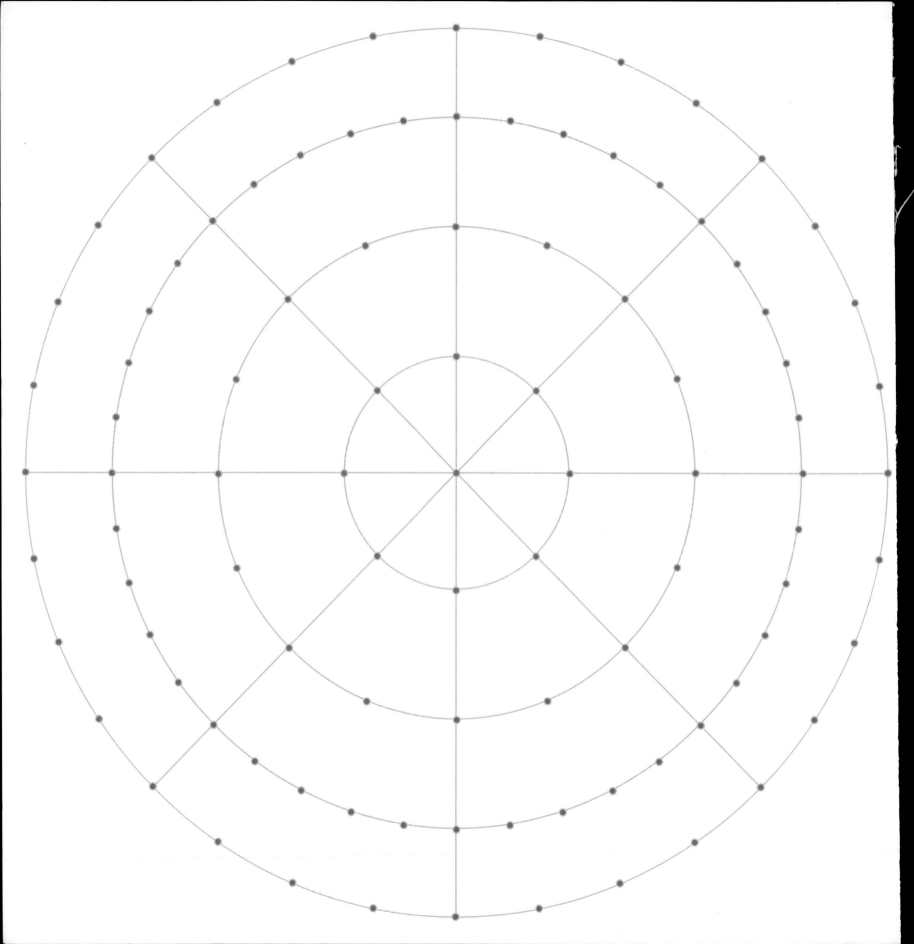

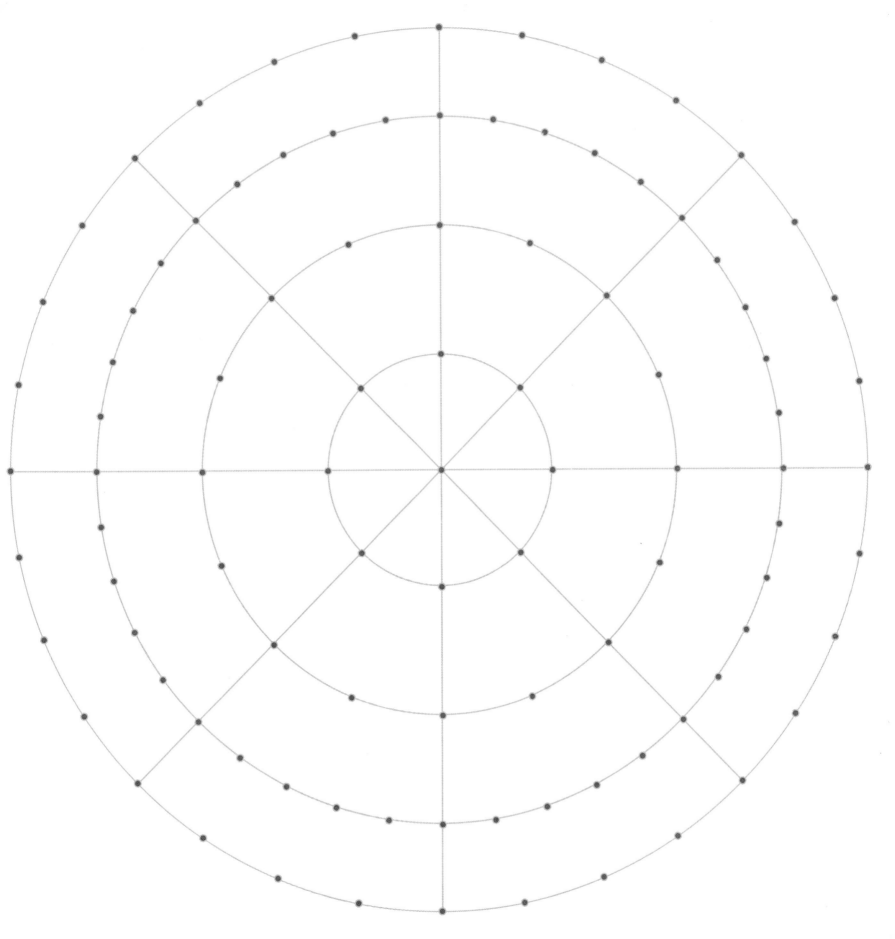

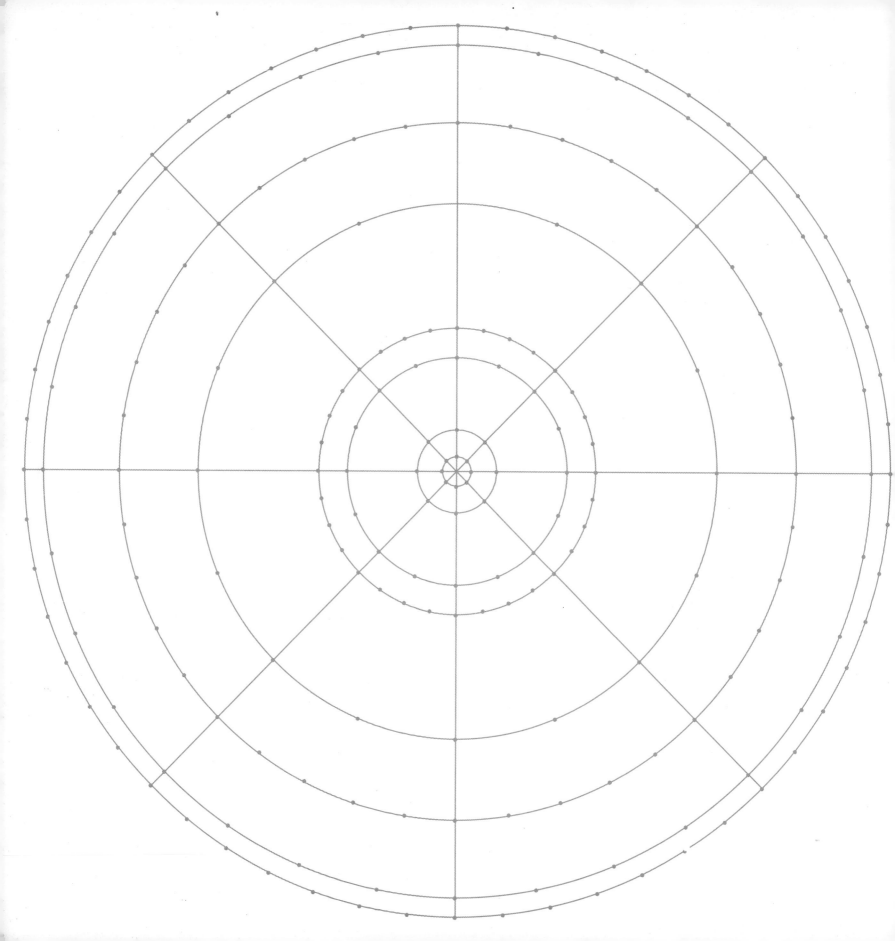